'I don't suppose very many of your clients flirt with you,' Elliot drawled suggestively.

'I really think that sort of thing isn't appropriate, given our circumstances…'

'Our circumstances?'

Was he laughing at her? 'I work for you,' Melissa elaborated uncomfortably.

'Oh, yes, of course you do. And I genuinely didn't want to make you uncomfortable, although…' He paused, and looked straight at her. 'Flirting is only dangerous if it gets out of hand.'

'Gets out of hand?' Melissa repeated nervously.

Cathy Williams is originally from Trinidad but has lived in England for a number of years. She currently has a house in Warwickshire, which she shares with her husband Richard, her three daughters Charlotte, Olivia and Emma, and their pet cat Salem. She adores writing romantic fiction and would love one of her girls to become a writer—although at the moment she is happy enough if they do their homework and agree not to bicker with one another.

Recent titles by the same author:

THE BILLIONAIRE BOSS'S BRIDE
THE ITALIAN TYCOON'S MISTRESS
HIS VIRGIN SECRETARY
THE GREEK TYCOON'S SECRET CHILD

IN THE BANKER'S BED

BY
CATHY WILLIAMS

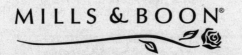

MILLS & BOON®

First published in Great Britain 2005
Harlequin Mills & Boon Limited,
Eton House, 18-24 Paradise Road, Richmond, Surrey TW9 1SR

© Cathy Williams 2005

ISBN 0 263 84139 1

Set in Times Roman 10½ on 11½ pt.
01-0405-53107

Printed and bound in Spain
by Litografia Rosés, S.A., Barcelona

CHAPTER ONE

ELLIOT frowned as he stared out of the window. The spacious, minimalist room had a particularly pleasing view over one of the few areas of greenery in London and, basking in the full light of a summer day, one would be forgiven for thinking that they were somewhere in the Med, and not, in fact, standing in a private room in a posh gym in central London.

Elliot glanced impatiently at his watch and swung round to face the door, leaning against the window-ledge.

Waiting was something Elliot Jay didn't do. It was something other people did. He expected his summons to be obeyed immediately without him having to hang around for…twenty minutes so far, according to his watch.

With mounting frustration, he stalked across to one of the chairs and sat down, wishing that he'd had the sense to bring his laptop with him so that he could at least do some work, wishing even more that he wasn't now in the position of having to do what he was doing, but he had no choice. Circumstances beyond his control had brought him to this juncture.

With a discipline born of experience, Elliot closed his mind off from those particularly unwelcome circumstances and instead allowed his eyes to roam around the room, to take in its harmonious lack of clutter, its sanitised impersonality. This was one of the reasons he had joined this particular gym when it had opened its doors eighteen months ago. That and the fact that it was a stone's throw from his massive penthouse apartment in

Kensington. Vigo was a health club that didn't waste time trying to be cosy. There were no chummy sitting-room-style bars where the weary could unwind with gossip over cups of tea, no lounging chairs around the pool or wavy slides for the kiddies. Instead the bars were all kitted out just like this room, in black and chrome with sensible newspapers on the tables. There was an internet café for anyone inclined to stay longer than was strictly necessary and the exercise machines were of the highest specification. Not that he used them. He unwound twice a week over a brutal game of squash and then swam it off in the giant-sized pool which, at eight in the evening, was usually empty.

As in every area of his life, Elliot applied himself to his exercise with focused, ruthless concentration. As a teenager, his skills on the rugby field had been formidable enough to warrant encouragement from his coach to turn professional, not that being a professional sportsman had ever presented itself as a practical possibility. His intellect could never have been contained by something as physically demanding as a sport, however talented he might have been at it. His finely tuned brain required enormous mental challenge. As the youngest ever chairman of a prominent investment bank, not only did he get this challenge, but he also earned the phenomenal sums of money associated with the job, which meant that by the age of thirty-two he could afford to begin indulging in his own private ventures, which brought their own financial rewards. The intense workload, which most men would have found crippling, Elliot found invigorating. His days were charged with adrenaline and mapped out with the precision of military campaigns. Meetings followed meetings and his name was synonymous with thrusting success in the financial world.

But Elliot didn't work for the money. He worked because he was driven. Even his hours of relaxation had a purpose.

Right now, he had a task at hand and hanging around wasn't something he found relaxing. In fact, he had to curb his annoyance and remember that in this one instance, he was actually in the unfamiliar terrain of the supplicant asking a favour.

Which didn't mean that he liked it.

But Melissa Lee had been personally recommended to him by the manager of the gym, a shrewd businesswoman and someone he trusted to give him clear-headed, impartial advice. Of course, he had been sparing with the actual details, merely told her that he required someone who could assist someone slightly overweight and a bit off-key. The Lee woman fitted the bill to the detail. She was twenty-four, a nutritionist and physiotherapist by training, although more than capable of mapping out a successful exercise routine, and she was fairly new to the gym, so had not yet acquired a string of regulars who needed her attention on a regular basis.

Keen though he was to employ Melissa Lee for the task at hand, he still could not resist looking pointedly at his watch when she finally entered the room.

'I've been waiting for forty minutes, Miss Lee.'

Melissa looked at the figure casually reclining on the chair and stopped abruptly in her tracks.

'One of our clients is interested in seeing you about a personal job,' Samantha had told her, interrupting the session which Melissa had only just started. 'Right now, if you could possibly make it.' Samantha had failed to elaborate on either the nature of the job or the nature of the client in question, and the *right now* command in the sentence Melissa had chosen tactfully to ignore.

The blood now rushed to Melissa's face as she took in the physically striking specimen in front of her.

Working in a gym was a passport to seeing impressively built men. Every morning, when Melissa went in for her light workout on the machines at seven-thirty, before she began her daily routines, they were there, suits waiting for them in changing rooms while they primed themselves for the day ahead on rowing machines and treadmills and other vicious-looking instruments of torture. From the relatively relaxed safety of an exercise mat, she absentmindedly watched them as she did her sit-ups, knowing herself to be unobserved because it had to be said that most of them had eyes only for themselves in the floor-to-ceiling mirrors that dominated the massive rooms.

But she had never seen the man sitting in front of her before. She would have remembered if she had. He had a memorable face. Glossy raven-black hair contrasted vividly with his eyes, which were a pure, cold blue, and his bone structure was perfect enough to make her do a double take. He was a sensationally attractive male, and even in that split second of taking him in she knew that he possessed the kind of presence that most women would have buckled at the knees at.

His expression, however, did not encourage that reaction in her. In fact, Melissa felt her smile rapidly fade away and she became aware that she was hovering by the door, like a student called in to see the headmaster for cheating in class.

She drew in her breath and took a few assertive steps into the room, holding out her hand, noticing that, although he politely extended his to briefly take hers, he didn't budge from his position on the chair, instead gesturing for her to sit down, as though he owned the place.

'I take it you are Miss Lee?' Blue eyes roved at a leisurely pace over her.

'That's right,' Melissa answered, disconcerted by his

scrutiny. 'I'm sorry if I've kept you waiting but I was in the middle of a session when Samantha told me that you wanted to see me.' She found no smiling acceptance of her apology, rather, silence and those ice-blue eyes appraising her, as though committing how she looked to memory. It was destabilising. Was he aware of that? 'She said that you wanted to see me about a job of some kind.' Whatever job it was, she decided on the spot that she wasn't going to take it. The man was positively intimidating. He also didn't look as though he needed any extra help with working out. Even dressed as he was in casual trousers and short-sleeved shirt, she could see that his body was well-toned and muscular with a slightly bronzed hue that gave him an exotic, compelling beauty. If he did want extra help working out, then it would be to a calibre that she, for one, was not trained to supply.

'That's right, although, of course, should you get this particular job, then showing up late would be out of the question.'

'I *did* apologise,' Melissa muttered in self-defence. 'You could hardly expect me to cancel Mrs Evans without notice just because I had to suddenly dash over here to see you. Mrs Evans is one of my few regular clients and she really needs the physiotherapy sessions she has with me twice a week. She was in a car accident a few months ago and—'

'Enough.' Elliot held up one hand impatiently. 'I'm not here to waste time talking about perfect strangers. I'm here to put forward a proposal which I think you will find financially very rewarding.'

Still smarting from having effectively been told to shut up, Melissa drew herself up and surveyed him loftily. 'I'm employed by Vigo, Mr…Mr…I don't know your name…'

'Jay. You can call me Elliot.'

She preferred not to call him anything. 'I don't think I would be allowed to take on outside work. I'm sure there must be something in my contract about that. Besides, I have a pretty hectic schedule at the moment and it's increasing by the day. I may only have been here a few months but...'

'You needn't worry about taking time off for this job. No objections will be raised, I assure you.' He was beginning to wonder what had possessed Samantha to sing the praises of this woman. She certainly wasn't what he had expected. For one thing, he hadn't expected to have to argue his case. He didn't know how much newcomers earned at a gym, but he would bet his bottom dollar that it wasn't a fortune, and London was an expensive place to live in. The prospect of some extra money should have been greeted with howls of delight.

And for another thing, Melissa Lee wasn't physically what he had expected either. He couldn't see very much under her shapeless dress but what he did see didn't accord with someone in the business of the body beautiful. She clearly wasn't fat but neither was she whipcord-slender with the muscles to match. She also didn't look the sort who thrived on putting people through their paces. He suppressed a sigh of pure frustration.

'I expect you want to know about the job I have in mind?'

'I don't think I can help you,' Melissa informed him up front. 'You're obviously a regular here at the gym and, whatever kind of workout you may have in mind for yourself, you really would need someone more qualified in the area. You see, I'm not sure whether Samantha told you, but I'm employed primarily as a nutritionist and a physiotherapist. I do a few classes but that's with the over-sixties. Mostly stretching exercises, very light-weight. You could probably do those in your sleep.'

'Finished?' he enquired politely, when she had dried up. He waited for her absolute, undivided attention. 'Do you normally approach everything in such a negative manner? Spotting all the obstacles before you take one step forward? If so, then I feel very sorry for these clients of yours. Do they know what they're getting into? That you won't make them better but in fact will see every pitfall, point them out and then lead them to the nearest bridge so that they can jump off?'

'That's not fair!' Melissa's normally warm, sunny disposition abandoned her completely. This man was hateful. Cold, emotionless, forbidding, arrogant and *hateful*. She couldn't think of anything worse than helping him in any way, shape or form. Or even being exposed to him unnecessarily. The man should carry a health warning. She opened her mouth to tell him just that, but he spoke first.

'We seem to have got off on the wrong foot.' He leant forward to rest his elbows on his thighs and she distractedly took in the rippling of muscle under the thin shirt, the powerful arms lightly dusted with a sprinkling of dark hair. 'I'm not here to hire you for myself. I'm here to hire you for my daughter.'

Melissa's mouth fell open and she gaped. The man *had a daughter*? Yes, he looked virile. In fact, physically at least, he was every inch the alpha male, just the sort magazines had a habit of pointing out was the average fertile woman's subconscious dream man, the sort that sent fantasies of reproduction into overdrive.

Melissa tried to picture him as a father and failed.

'You look shocked,' Elliot pointed out politely. 'Am I stretching the bounds of your imagination here?'

'Yes,' Melissa squawked truthfully. 'You have a *daughter*? I'm sorry…it's just that you don't seem…

well…you don't strike me as the sort of man…not that there's a *sort*…of course not—'

Elliot interrupted. 'This is something of a long story. If you're interested in hearing about the job, then I suggest we meet at a more civilised time to discuss it. I *had* expected to have sorted this matter out tonight, but it's now nine-thirty and I assume you have to get home, so shall we say six tomorrow evening? In the bar downstairs?'

'Six tomorrow. Yes. Fine,' Melissa repeated, still struggling to take in the impossible fact that Elliot Jay was a father.

He stood up and stared down at her. 'And just in case you're inclined to gossip, don't. I abhor it. This will be a private arrangement between us and I won't want the details to be spread around this gym.'

'I don't gossip.' Her wide blue eyes met his and then she couldn't look away. She just kept staring until he nodded curtly at her and swung around, leaving her still gaping like a stranded goldfish.

'And make sure that you're here on time tomorrow. I'm a busy man.'

Really and truly, Melissa had had no intention of taking whatever job he had in mind. The financial carrot he had dangled in front of her had barely registered, even though it was true that money was tight. She had arrived in London six months previously, clutching her newly gained qualifications and with no real appreciation of the fact that prices in London were on a completely different scale from prices in the north. Everything, she had rapidly discovered, was more expensive, and the most expensive of all was the housing market.

Right now, Melissa rented a studio apartment in Shepherd's Bush, which had optimistically advertised itself as warm, cosy and perfect for the single professional non-smoker. In reality it was poky, basic and not perfect for anything that had a pulse. The bathroom and toilet facilities were shared, which was hideous, and the kitchen was so tiny that cooking anything more elaborate than pasta required juggling skills she didn't possess. Her salary at the gym covered the rent and left a bit over for living expenses, but her hard-saved cash was slowly expiring. However much she tried to rein in the spending, life was just expensive in London.

The financially lucrative side of the proposal should have struck a chord but it hadn't.

The mention of a daughter had struck the chord.

Curiosity, she reminded herself over and over during the course of the following day, killed the cat. So he had a daughter. Big deal. That didn't make him unique, it made him a statistic.

A very persistent statistic, she discovered. The image of his dark, cold face hovered at the edge of her mind, alternately sending chills down her spine and spiking her curiosity. Curious enough to find herself at the internet café during her lunch break, surfing the net for information about Elliot Jay.

There was a wealth of it.

Thirty-two years old, with an illustrious academic background, having boarded at Winchester College and then moved on to Oxford University, which he left with a first-class degree in law and economics. His rise to power was chartered succinctly, a little background preceding the onslaught of information on his current status as financial giant with a talent for reading market trends and betting audaciously on the outcome.

No mention, she noticed, eating a baguette and scanning down the pages and pages of information, most of which covered details of deals that didn't interest her, of any daughter. Or, for that matter, of any wife.

In fact, not much information about his personal background at all. She wondered whether he kept his wife and daughter locked away in a closet somewhere. Maybe the basement of his house, where they couldn't interfere in his life. He was, as he had said himself, *a very busy man.* Too busy for a family? They had probably come along at a time before his glittering career had taken shape and had since had to take a back seat to the deals and acquisitions. From what she read, the only thing the man seemed to do was work.

Or maybe, she thought, reluctantly switching off the computer, the daughter was a ruse to get her interested in whatever proposal he had in mind.

Melissa, despite her practical training, had a vibrant imagination. One wayward thought could spiral into a series of improbable scenarios which she savoured with childish enjoyment. Even she, though, couldn't see why someone like Elliot Jay might have concocted a daughter out of thin air for her benefit. Which meant the daughter must be real. Which spiked her curiosity even more. Which, in turn, meant that by a quarter to six she was waiting for Elliot Jay in the bar, nursing a glass of sparkling mineral water.

And she had even spent an unheard-of length of time in one of the plush ladies' rooms trying to do something with her appearance. Her hair was beyond control. Too blonde, too curly and too fond of doing its own thing, which usually involved staging an all-out rebellion against hair-clips and tie-backs. She had done her best with it, which meant tying it back as firmly as she could into something of a French plait. It was long enough to succumb to that attempt at restraint, but just not sleek enough to do so gracefully. As a result wispy tendrils floated around her face and it would have taken a bulk buy of hair grips to subdue them.

Her face, though, she had worked with. She had always thought that the advantage of having an ordinary face was that it could be made up to look less plain than it really was. And she had an ordinary face. There were no cheekbones you could cut with, no wide, full lips for a truly sensual look, no thatch of black eyelashes like those that always stared back at her in an unbelievably long manner from the pages of magazines advertising mascara. She had an oval face, blue eyes with no mysterious green flecks, a small, straight nose and a mouth that looked ready to smile at the slightest opportunity.

That about summed it up. She had applied some lip gloss and livened up her colour with some blusher. Her figure she had played down, just as she always had, ever since the age of thirteen when her curves and breasts had become an unwelcome focus of adolescent male attention. Her dress, just like the one she had worn the previous day, was functional and summery and twinned with a lightweight boxy jacket, and successfully managed to conceal most of her figure. At least the bits of it she didn't much like.

She sipped her water, feeling in control, and glanced down idly at the *Financial Times* resting on the small circular table in front of her. When she looked back up at the door, it was to see Elliot Jay framed in it, his sharp eyes glancing across the room and finding her.

Melissa felt her stomach go into brief, unpleasant free fall. If it was possible, he looked even more intimidating from a distance than he had from close up the night before. His body was long and elegant and muscular. His conventional grey suit should have disguised the fact but didn't. He looked like a sophisticated predator. From what she had read about him, he looked the way he was. A ruthless financier who had no time for the frivolous side of life. Did he ever laugh? For that matter, did his face ever crack into a smile?

He covered the distance between them while she was still staring at him.

'You're on time. Good.' He sat down and glanced at her.

'I usually *am* on time. You caught me off guard yesterday, as I explained.'

'You're drinking water. Is that to impress me or is it in accordance with your diet? I expect as a nutritionist you take your food very seriously.'

'I didn't think I had to impress you, Mr Jay.'

'Elliot.'

'Elliot. And I'm drinking water because getting sloshed on wine in the bar of the health club I work in doesn't seem appropriate.' Melissa could feel every nerve in her body standing to attention.

'No, I don't suppose it does. Least of all if you're a nutritionist by profession. Samantha gave me a bit of background about you. Perhaps you'd like to fill me in yourself?'

For one dizzy minute, she thought that he was asking her about her private life, inviting her to launch into an explanation of what she did aside from working at Vigo, but then common sense kicked in. The man wanted to put a deal to her and he needed to find out what qualifications she had and what her experience was.

'Don't you think you should tell me what the job is that you have in mind for me first? Then, if it sounds promising, I can go through my work experience with you.'

Elliot sat forward, his body shifting only by a matter of a few inches, but enough for Melissa's instincts to shriek in alarm and cause her to pull back.

'Let's get one thing straight, Miss Lee; I ask the questions. You provide the information.'

'That sounds like a democratic process,' Melissa commented blandly and for just one second she caught astonishment in his eyes. Surprise that she had dared respond to something that didn't invite a response.

'I'm glad you agree,' he said coolly. 'Now I'm going to get something for myself to drink. Would you like another...water?'

'Oh, no. I find one glass is enough for me. Another one and it might just start tasting medicinal.' She waggled her glass at him and in return he nodded in a clipped fashion before stalking off to the bar. Noticeable how the bartender scurried over to him, she thought wryly. Must come with being an autocrat.

As soon as he sat back down she handed him her CV, which she had thought to bring only at the last minute. Elliot read it quickly, put it on the table between them and sat back in the chair, nursing a glass of white wine.

'Good A levels but no university degree. How come?'

Well, he *was* a *very busy man*. No time for any polite leads into the interrogation process.

'I decided to take a year out in America. The easiest way was down the au pair route and I enjoyed the work so much that I returned to England and put the degree on hold.'

'That would imply that getting a degree wasn't of any great importance in the first place.'

Melissa shrugged. 'I thought you were going to ask questions. You didn't tell me that you were going to put your own interpretation on the answers.'

Elliot felt another surge of frustration, like an itch in the middle of his back, which he just couldn't reach to scratch. 'It's part and parcel of getting to know you, which I believe is part of the point of an interview...'

'For a job which I may or may not accept.'

He resisted a sigh. 'Why did you decide to switch from nannying to physiotherapy?' His eyes roamed unconsciously down her body and came up against the immutable barrier of another flowered dress. This time the flowers were smaller and closer together. It reminded him of a quilt cover used by one of his girlfriends many years ago. He stopped his lazy, hooded inspection to listen to her telling him about the switch in her career path, explaining that she had always taken a keen interest in the practical workings of the body, that it had seemed a sensible thing to do in terms of a long-term career. The course had been up north and she had been able to live with her parents while she did it, so that the money accumulated from her nannying days could be saved.

'Thank goodness,' she was explaining now in what struck him as a very melodic voice for someone so drab. 'The cost of living in London is ridiculous. Have you any idea what sort of prices landlords are charging for rooms? No, I don't suppose you have. Well, a lot. Just in case you ever feel the need to know.'

Elliot relaxed. Money. Whoever said it wasn't the universal language? Never mind the hard-to-get, I-just-might-turn-your-offer-down approach she was taking. She needed the money, just as he had expected.

'Shocking,' he drawled. 'Samantha has a high opinion of you. Says you're reliable, you know what you're talking about and you're prepared to take on new challenges. She also says that you're very good with people.' *Forthright* might have been a better word, he thought.

Melissa's face dimpled into a smile. 'I like to think so, but it's very nice knowing that someone else agrees.'

The smile gave her face a radiance that now matched her voice and for a few seconds he was a little taken aback.

Like all facets of his life, women were neatly slotted into a category. Not that he ran through them at a rate of knots. He didn't. The lifestyle of a workaholic could not accommodate the lifestyle of a playboy and there had never been any question of making the choice. He dated women as driven as himself. They had always been high-ranking professionals and the conversation was always invigorating. It was an eye-opener and damned useful to see how the female population considered business problems, to understand the angle they came from.

And right now…

Elliot glanced down at his watch. He still had time. He wouldn't be meeting Alison for another hour and a half, a rare treat to meet her so early in the evening, and on a weekday, when one or the other of them, more often than not both, just wouldn't have been able to get away.

'Do you enjoy your job?' he asked suddenly, switching his thoughts from his date.

'Of course I do.'

'What I have in mind would require your full attention, at least from four in the afternoon onwards. You might also be asked to report for duty on some mornings, probably around seven.'

'Report for duty.' She gave him a quizzical smile.

'That's about it essentially. Naturally, there would be no need for you to carry on working here while in my employ, as the salary would be for a full-time position, but you might want to continue with some of your clients during the day when you had free time. The weekends, I'm afraid, might involve work but overall I don't think the position would be for longer than three months.'

Sick of pussyfooting around, Melissa decided to take the bull by the horns. 'I looked you up on the internet. During my lunch break. I found lots of stuff about you but not a word about your wife or daughter.'

'I don't have a wife.'

'Oh. Divorced?'

The question met with a cold look of disapproval and Melissa raised her shoulders apologetically before he could launch into an attack on her nosiness. 'OK. I can tell from the expression on your face that the question was out of bounds. Am I right? No personal curiosity?'

'You got it in one,' Elliot grated.

'Because you hold the monopoly on asking questions. Am I right there as well? No, don't bother to answer that one. Tell me about your daughter, about the job. Not,' she felt constrained to add, 'that there's any guarantee that I'll take it…'

'Even though you obviously need the money?' Elliot said silkily. He named the figure he had in mind and watched with great satisfaction as she did a double take. 'Thought so,' he said softly. 'Too good to pass up, wouldn't you say? Especially when you consider that the job would leave you more or less free to carry on with whatever regular clients you've managed to recruit at the gym…'

Melissa looked at him with dislike. 'Not everyone is driven by money.'

'True. But most can be persuaded into accepting it.' A cool, cynical smile curved his mouth.

'What's your daughter's name and why is there no mention of her in any of the articles I read about you on the internet? Is there something wrong with her?'

The humourless smile vanished, replaced by a frown. 'No, there's nothing wrong with her, at least not in the sense I think you mean.' He had finished his drink and stood up. 'I need another one of these. You? Still going to stick to the mineral water because it just wouldn't do to be seen drinking alcohol in the health club bar?'

The way he said it made it sound like a challenge. Too

big a challenge to resist, especially when it was coming from him. 'OK. I'll have a white wine too.'

'So,' he said, minutes later when he had resumed his seat, 'about my daughter. I'll start with the easy bit. Her name's Lucy and she's fourteen years old.'

'Fourteen!' Melissa tried to do some rapid maths in her head. He would have been a teenager when he'd become a father! A young, hopeful husband with life stretching out before him with its infinite promise. Except he wasn't divorced, which meant that he had never married the woman who had fallen pregnant with his child.

'I see you've worked out the sums,' Elliot drawled, sipping the wine and looking at her over the rim of his glass. He seemed to be the master of the unreadable expression. There he sat, presenting her with this extraordinary fact, and there wasn't a flicker of emotion on his face. No wonder she felt so hot and bothered around him, she told herself, she just wasn't used to this level of emotionless coldness.

'I was at university when I met Rebecca. She was over from Australia doing her Masters in psychology. I was an undergraduate doing my degree in law and economics.' He paused and looked at her assessingly. 'Talking about my private life isn't something I'm accustomed to doing, but there seems to be no choice at the moment.' He carefully placed the glass on the table and linked his fingers together on his lap.

'Everybody has a private life,' Melissa said in bewilderment. 'I don't suppose anyone is interested in yours any more than you're interested in theirs.'

'In case you hadn't noticed, I'm not just *anyone*.'

Melissa looked for arrogance behind the remark, but surprisingly there was none. He was stating a fact.

'I know you're important, but you're still a human being.'

'An intensely private one. I do my utmost to keep my personal profile low. I'm telling you this because…'

'You think that the minute you walk out of here, I might just run around the gym spreading the salacious news. Not to mention going to a few of the tabloids and trying to flog the story.'

For the first time he smiled. Reluctantly but appreciatively. A genuine smile that knocked her sideways for a few suffocating seconds because it changed the harsh contours of his face. She had a glimpse of the sexy man underneath the ruthless, cold business machine and it was like receiving an electric shock.

She dodged her confusion in a quick gulp of wine. 'I won't. Believe it or not, I am a professional and I don't blab. Not that I would blab even if I wasn't a professional. So you had a fling when you were still a kid and discovered that the fling had slightly more permanent consequences than you'd anticipated.'

'Not really, no.'

'But you just said…'

'Yes, I had a fling. She was twenty-seven to my eighteen. Lust met opportunity and…' He looked at her from under his lashes, expecting comprehension, and Melissa nodded, head inclined to one side.

Lust meeting opportunity was a situation she had personally never encountered. Friendship meeting curiosity, yes, she'd experienced two of those, both short-lived and amicable in their endings. Lust, on the other hand, was something of an alien concept. She glanced at that brooding, darkly handsome face and shivered.

'And…?'

CHAPTER TWO

'AND a relationship was born.' He shrugged.

Eyes wide, Melissa leant forward and looked at him with frowning concentration. 'You make it sound like a mathematical equation. Didn't it mean anything to you?'

Elliot clicked his tongue dismissively. 'This isn't about what that relationship meant to me. It's about dealing with the consequences of it.' When she looked at him like that, big blue eyes wide with interest, it was like being gazed at by a puppy. He suppressed his irritation and brought the subject unequivocally back to the matter in hand. 'The point is that what we had lasted six months or thereabouts. It was fun but it was never destined to last.'

'Who broke it off?'

This time he snapped and leaned towards her with an aggressive thrust of his jaw. 'It doesn't matter. Can you understand that? The details are irrelevant! The fact is that Rebecca returned to Australia with no forwarding address. I never knew she was pregnant. Until, that is, six months ago, when I was contacted by my lawyer and informed I had a daughter.'

Melissa's mouth opened in shock. 'What happened?'

'What happened was a road accident. Rebecca and her husband were apparently both dead by the time the ambulance got to the scene.'

'How awful.'

'Yes, I imagine it was,' Elliot conceded. 'The bald truth of the matter, however, is that Rebecca was an only child. Her only living relative close to her was her

23

mother, who lives in an old people's home in Melbourne and Brian...well, her husband had an assortment of relatives, none of whom he was particularly close to. He was English and hadn't actually returned to this country for nearly fourteen years.'

'And how did they...find out about...well, *you*?'

'I was named on the birth certificate, for a start. It was also lodged in their joint will that should anything happen to them, I was to be contacted.'

He was relaying a string of facts. His face, as Melissa stared at him, was unreadable. She felt an unexpected pang of sympathy for him. She felt an even bigger surge of compassion for his daughter, abruptly having to face the loss of her mother and stepfather as well as the disorientation of finding herself in another country, far from home and the familiar things she had grown up with.

With sudden impulse, she reached out to put her hand on his wrist and their eyes met. He didn't physically withdraw his hand, but he might just as well have because his eyes were cool and unwelcoming.

'There's no need to feel sorry for me. It's a situation that has to be dealt with, which is where you come in.'

Melissa removed her hand as though she had been stung.

'Lucy hasn't settled in very well over here.'

'Can you blame her?'

'Of course not. But that doesn't change the reality of the situation. She's at a school she claims to loathe, she takes refuge in her bedroom whenever she can and she eats. She's put on quite a bit of weight since she arrived on my doorstep five months ago and there's no sign of her breaking out of the pattern.'

'And what do you want me to do about it?' Melissa asked, bewildered. Couldn't he see that that was a problem he had to sort out himself?

'Put her on some kind of controlled diet, encourage her to do some exercise.'

'But…'

'Does the job appeal to you or not? It's as simple a question as that. If not, then I won't waste my time further.'

'It's not really about whether the job appeals or not,' Melissa felt obliged to explain, even though his expression wasn't encouraging. 'It's about whether I would be of any use…well, in a situation like that. It seems to be a very complex one and…'

'All situations, complex or not, have solutions. Cut away the waffle and the psychobabble and there is always a solution, and the easiest solutions are usually the most effective.'

'That might work in the world of business,' Melissa retorted, 'but it doesn't work when it comes to real life.'

'As I said, problems have solutions. Being naïve and emotional doesn't get anyone very far in coming up with the solutions. Now, are you prepared to take this job on?'

Was she? Was she prepared to have anything further to do with this man? He was as unfeeling as a block of ice and working for him would be a lesson in endurance, which was something that didn't feature highly on her list of *must do* experiences.

On the other hand, her imagination was stirred at the thought of his daughter.

She nodded silently.

'Right. Then let's get down to business.' He reached inside the pocket of his lightweight jacket and produced an envelope, from which he extracted a sheet of paper. 'It's a contract,' he said shortly, interpreting her bemused expression. 'It lays out all the terms of conditions of this placement. You just need to sign…there.' One long finger pointed to the bottom and he handed her a pen that was as classy as his clothes and his watch and his shoes and everything else about him.

'Is a contract really necessary?' Melissa asked dubiously. 'I mean, we can keep things informal...'

'We could. But we won't.'

She reluctantly took the pen, signed on the dotted line and wondered what she was signing herself up for.

'Good. I'll hang on to your CV so that I have all the details of your address and phone number, and a copy of this will be sent to you tomorrow. I've spoken to Samantha and she'll release you whenever you feel free to start. My preference is for next Monday. That way you'll have a couple of days to readjust your appointments because your day here will effectively end by three-thirty, in time to meet Lucy from school.'

'You want her to exercise *every day*?'

'That might work.' He hesitated, thinking about what he was going to say next, how he was going to phrase his intentions. 'I'm not talking about gruelling workouts...'

'Oh, I doubt I could oblige there anyway...' Melissa couldn't resist grinning. 'My workouts are strictly geared towards the less energetic...'

The grin was infectious. Not that Elliot was inclined to grin back. He did, however, find himself slightly put off his stride. 'Why would you choose to work at a health club if you don't like exercising?'

'Oh, I never said that I didn't *like* it. In small doses, exercise is good fun. But intense workouts don't do a great deal for me. And to answer your question, I came here to work because it offered an interesting clientele and the surroundings are terrific. Also, it was the first place to offer me a job.'

'Interesting clientele...'

'Yes. This place is popular with lots of sports people.

I get a fair amount of practice working with sporting injuries.' She paused and looked at him curiously. 'What do *you* do here?'

'Squash,' Elliot said abruptly. He suddenly realised that he had swerved off the subject. Time was moving on. He glanced down at his watch. 'Twice a week if I'm lucky. It's fast, it's furious and it's competitive.'

Three things that a man like this one would relish, she thought, particularly the competitive aspect of it. Swimming could be fast and furious but then it would lack that essential ingredient of pitting one's skills against someone else.

'Which is beside the point,' he said, snapping her out of her speculations. 'The point is that the job would involve slightly more than a simple diet sheet and some light sit-ups.' He sighed heavily, the first sign of any human emotion, and leant forward, elbows resting on his thighs. 'I would want you to motivate my daughter. I am not utterly insensitive. I understand she's going through a very difficult time but I am rarely around at civilised hours. I have an intensely demanding job.'

'What do you mean by *motivate*?'

'Take her jogging now and again in the park, maybe followed by something to eat afterwards. Introduce her to some of the shops. Naturally you will have a bank account opened for you and a credit card issued so that there will be no necessity to think about the money aspect of it.'

'But...'

'I'm coming to that. It all might eat into your private life, hence the substantial salary I'm offering. However, it will be of a limited time duration. I'm sure whatever boyfriend you might have in the background could adjust for a short while.' Actually, he hadn't really considered whether she had a boyfriend or not. Now he found himself wondering what sort of boy he would be, should she have one. She seemed spectacularly unimpressed by material things, so he imagined someone fairly run of the mill, a nice, unchallenging lad, the kind that mums and dads up and down the land would love to see their daughters bring home.

'It's not a question of a boyfriend…'

'No one around on the scene? That's good.'

'Which isn't to say that I don't have a social life,' Melissa informed him, feeling like someone trying to swim against a strong current.

'Which isn't to say that I have implied that,' Elliot said, gravely mimicking her turn of expression. 'All I am saying is that some flexibility might be required and I'm sure I can leave that in your hands. All you need do is to show up at my place next Monday at, let's say, four? Lucy should be back from school by then and if not Lenka can always let you in.'

'Lenka?'

'My Polish housekeeper. She's there every day.'

And that was it? End of discussion? She could see that he was getting ready to leave.

'And what about *you*?' she squeaked urgently, and was granted a puzzled look.

'What about me?'

'Are you in touch with Planet Earth? I mean, I know you're a bigwig in the City and you're probably used to snapping your fingers and having everyone jump to attention without asking any questions, but that's just not how it works in a situation like this!'

Elliot opened his mouth to speak. No one, but *no one* talked to him like this! Least of all someone he was about to employ and on a damned good salary besides! Although the remark about him snapping his fingers did carry a certain element of truth. He swallowed back his immediate impulse and looked at her coolly and politely.

'I can't just present myself to your daughter when she gets back from school. She won't have a clue what to do and neither will I.'

'Naturally I will forewarn her of your arrival.'

'By telling her what?'

'By telling her that you've been employed to help her work on an exercise and diet programme.' He shrugged. 'It seems pretty straightforward to me.'

'Well, it might seem straightforward to *you*, but it doesn't seem straightforward to *me*.' She stuck her chin out and braced herself to rush headlong into the full blast of his disapproval. 'And furthermore, there will be no question of my taking this job unless I get a little co-operation from you!'

'Feel free to explain,' Elliot said in a withering voice.

'You need to be there when I am introduced to your daughter! It's going to be an awkward moment and you might just want to get the arrangement off to a good start by smoothing things over from the beginning!'

'Smoothing things over…' He laughed mirthlessly. 'I think you've picked the wrong candidate for that particular job. In the past five months I can say with my hand on my heart that smoothing things over with Lucy is something I have abundantly failed to achieve. However, I'll make sure that I'm there to do the introductions.' He stood up. 'I'm afraid I really have to leave you now. Is there anything else you need to know?'

All the surface details were in place, but there was so much else Melissa felt she needed to know that she was stuck for words. She got to her feet and shook her head with a little laugh. 'Nothing that you'll probably feel inclined to tell me.'

'Meaning?' Elliot asked, turning away and heading for the door, which he proceeded to hold open for her.

'I suppose meaning how you feel about all of this, not just the practical issues involved. Meaning what your daughter is really like, as opposed to your description of her as an unhappy teenager who happened to find herself at your door one day. Meaning where you'd like things to end up, where you'd like to see your relationship with your daughter heading. It must be very hard for you, but you must have some thoughts about all of that stuff…'

'You're right,' Elliot said flatly, barely pausing in his stride towards the exit to spare her a brief look. 'There are no answers there that I feel inclined to tell you. I'll see you on Monday at four. Till then.' He nodded curtly in her direction and she watched as he disappeared from sight.

He'd vanished with a contract signed by her for a job which she was grappling to understand. On the surface, it bore all the hallmarks of a business arrangement, but scratch the surface and she knew that there was nothing businesslike about it at all. Whether he wanted to admit it or not, this arrangement was anchored in emotion. The emotions of an adolescent she didn't know and wasn't sure would even like *her*.

Why on earth would an unhappy, displaced teenager want to throw herself with delight into a diet and exercise routine with a perfect stranger? Someone employed by a man who was her father by blood only? Would she see it as a helpful gesture on the part of a newly found father trying to understand, or an insult from someone who couldn't be bothered to take time out to sort the situation?

The latter, she assumed, if Lucy was an ordinary mortal and not someone blessed with supernatural powers of insight. Elliot Jay was a study in coldness and if he intimidated *her*, then lord only knew what kind of effect he had on his daughter.

The thoughts ran round and round in her head for the remainder of the week and over the weekend, like little mice scurrying around in a cage. The worst of it was the fact that not only did she have to deal with a situation that was beginning to look like a disaster in the making, but also there was no one she could share the problem with.

Elliot had cautioned against gossip, which ruled out talking to all the people she knew at the gym, and she even felt treacherous thinking about asking an opinion from any of her friends she had left behind up north.

In the end she phoned her mum and after the usual pleasantries, which always included the key question about whether she was eating properly, she hesitatingly confided that she had managed to land a job outside working hours at the gym.

'Job? What kind of job?'

Melissa instantly regretted her foolhardy impulse to confide, least of all in her mother. Mothers, she belatedly thought, fussed, and her mother was the queen of fussers. How could she have forgotten all those anxious phone calls when she had been in America, checking to make sure that her baby was all right and hadn't been abducted by any stray perverts?

'Oh, as a nutritionist and exercise trainer,' Melissa said vaguely, plopping herself on the uncomfortable sofa that doubled up as a bed. She pictured her adorable mother, with her short, fluffy hair, frowning in concern. Imagination was definitely an inherited family trait. Thank goodness her father would be in later to spread some of his common sense and reason.

'Why would you need to do that outside normal working hours?'

'It's for a girl. A teenager. Her dad is a bit concerned about her eating habits. He's employed me to help out after school. Now and again.'

'Why on earth would he do that? Why not just get the child to join the gym?'

'Because…' Melissa tried to find a perfectly sensible answer to a perfectly sensible question… 'it's a question of transport,' she answered eventually. 'London isn't like home, Mum. There are tubes and trains and hundreds of buses…' That much was true at any rate, and she could almost hear her mother thinking that perhaps there was a little sense in that. The thought of teenagers and the underground system didn't go hand in hand in her mother's mind. Since she'd never been to London, her ideas of the transport system there were riddled with inaccuracies, only some of which Melissa had been able to put to rest.

'I can understand why a concerned father might not want his teenage girl to use public transport, I suppose.'

'And the salary's fantastic.' Which brought a new host of concerns. Why was this man paying her so much? She hoped there was no hidden agenda there! Melissa should know that men could be very underhand!

Melissa half listened, half thought about Elliot. His face was strangely recurring. In fact, she realised that she had been thinking of very little else for the past few days. She grinned to herself, listening to her mother, at the thought of how her mother would react should Melissa tell her that there was a man on her mind. She didn't think that Elliot and her parents would get along very well. They were a traditional, homely couple who enjoyed the simple things in life. He was…the opposite. She tried to imagine him as a homely type and had to stifle her laughter. He was about as homely as a charging rhino.

The phone call, even though she had said nothing much about the job, helped. Just talking to her mother helped. She just had to imagine her sensible, loving, supremely normal childhood to get everything else into perspective.

As a result, Melissa arrived at his apartment block on Monday at four precisely, still in an upbeat frame of mind.

Only as she stood outside, staring up at the white-fronted converted Georgian house, did her heart begin to fall.

She had thought to bring some books on diets and foods, a couple of easy-reading ones that a teenager might not find too offensive. She had been careful in choosing them, not wanting to look like someone who solved a body-odour problem in a colleague by giving them deodorant for a birthday present.

It had seemed an optimistic plan this morning. Now she felt horribly inexperienced to tackle what was hiding under the superficial problem. She took a deep breath and entered the building. There were no name-plates on the outside behind little plastic windows. She discovered the reason as soon as she walked inside. This was no ordinary converted house. Several houses had been knocked into one complete apartment block. Most of the ground floor consisted of an enormous porter's block and beyond that stretched gleaming flagstone tiles with sofas discreetly dispersed amongst large, abnormally healthy-looking plants.

There were two porters behind the shiny oak desk. One of them immediately and sharply asked whether he could help and Melissa tentatively approached, gave her name and asked for Mr Jay.

'Oh, yes. You must be Miss Lee. Mr Jay is expecting you. I'll just ring up.'

They both kept an eye on her while she looked around. Even the atmosphere in the place seemed different, smelled different. There was the smell of extreme wealth as opposed, she thought, to the vague smell of boiled cabbage that always greeted her whenever she walked into her block of flats. The exquisite flooring and the giant plants also helped with the impression. When she walked into the tiny hallway of her place, there wasn't a plant to be seen, never mind ones that looked as though they could swallow people whole, and the flooring was tired, cheap and stained round edges which had not seen any form of cleaning fluid for years.

'The lifts are through to the right,' the porter informed her, pointing. 'Straight up to the fourth floor.'

'Tell me,' Melissa said confidentially, 'how on earth do you manage to get your plants to look so healthy? I mean, are they *real*?'

It was an irresistible question for the plump porter, whose face had not cracked into a smile since the minute she had stepped through the door.

'Real,' he said in a triumphant voice. 'Chose them myself. The company that maintains the place wanted to have them provided by one of those plant firms but I persuaded them to let me have a go at kitting the place out. Bit of a plant fanatic, I am.' He leaned towards her. 'Just between you and me, I would love to move out to the country, get to see a bit of nature. Not much of that in London, I'm afraid.'

That made her think of her own home. Before she knew it she was chatting to him, telling him about the Yorkshire landscape, its rugged beauty, telling him about the orchids her father painstakingly cultivated.

'I haven't inherited his magic touch, though,' she finished sadly, thinking of her own efforts to brighten up her bedsit with one or two flowering plants. After their initial burst of good health, the flowers had all dropped off and all that remained were leaves. The leaves were thriving but defeated the purpose since she had wanted colour.

She left for the lift with the offer of a gardening book on its way.

With her cheerful frame of mind back in place, she headed up and was disgorged with a ping into a plushly carpeted hall. Two large blue and white urns greeted her, sandwiching a massive oval mirror, just right for checking her appearance, which, as usual, was not inspiring.

Not quite sure what to wear to win over an unhappy adolescent, Melissa had chosen a pair of casual cream-coloured trousers and a knitted cotton short-sleeved top with broad stripes. Now, inspecting herself in the conveniently placed mirror, she realised that the top was a tad too tight for her liking. Well, too tight given the size of her chest, which really needed camouflaging if her breasts weren't to stick out the way they were doing now, making all sorts of statements. And the broad horizontal stripes weren't too flattering either. Broad horizontal stripes, she decided glumly, should only be worn by very tall women who weighed under eight stone.

'Finished?' a voice enquired politely from somewhere to her right and Melissa jumped. 'Not that I want to rush you in any way, of course.' Elliot emerged fully from the doorway and stood there, inspecting her with his arms folded.

'I was about to knock on the door,' she said, her face bright red with embarrassment. 'Well, one of them.'

'Lucy's not back from school as yet.' He stood aside so that she could walk past him and a tingling feeling feathered through her as she brushed past him.

After the impressive entrance hall, Melissa was expecting more of the same from Elliot's apartment. She wasn't disappointed. This was truly an eye-opener into how the other half lived. The flat was open plan and stretched the entire length of the converted houses. There was no carpeting in sight. Just gleaming wood liberally scattered with richly coloured rugs. The sitting area was casual, with long, low sofas picking up the reds of the rugs and the kitchen was a marvel of avant-garde creativity. Towards the back, a short, curving staircase with wrought-iron banisters led up to what she could plainly see was an office. She could just about make out the bookshelves, the desk and the compulsory computer. In the little niche below the staircase was a small sitting area with a plasma-screen TV.

And away to both sides corridors led to other rooms. Bedrooms and bathrooms, she presumed.

When she finally swivelled back round to look at Elliot, it was to find his blue eyes on her and something very nearly like amusement on his face.

'Don't blame me for staring,' Melissa said with a grin. 'It's not every day that a working-class gal finds herself in a place like this.'

'Approve, do you?'

He hadn't expected to feel as gratified as he was feeling now at her reaction. When, after all, had been the last time someone had entered his apartment and had been so obviously bowled over? God, he couldn't remember! Money was a huge insulator. He mixed in circles where splendid apartments and country retreats were the norm. People didn't merely take holidays, they had travelling experiences, and because luxury was so readily available, curiosity and wonder were reactions of the past.

'It's absolutely…well…magnificent.' Melissa giggled nervously. 'Should I take my shoes off? What if I scuff all this expensive flooring?'

'What if you do?' Elliot drawled. 'No, you can keep your shoes on. They're nice, flat, sensible shoes. Very wood-flooring friendly.'

'That's me. Sensible.' She glanced down at her footwear, suddenly not much liking the fact that they were practical. 'It doesn't work wearing high heels when you have to travel on the underground. Too uncomfortable. What happens down the corridors?'

'What do you mean?'

'I mean, what's on either side?'

'You really can stop hovering there by the door.' He pushed himself off and headed towards the kitchen. 'Bedrooms and bathrooms happen. Six of the former and three of the latter. Do you want something to drink while we wait for Lucy to get home? Tea? Coffee?'

'Coffee would be fine. Thank you.' Should she go and sit on one of the sofas, she wondered, or should she join him in the kitchen, where bar stools were perched under the curving counter? Bar stool. Less formal. Plus she wouldn't have to shout to him while he rustled about in the kitchen doing something clever with a machine that looked as though it would be at home on a spaceship.

She hadn't banked on being quite as mesmerised by the movement of his hands as she watched him fiddle with the machine. She cupped her chin in the palm of her hand and stared, only launching into conversation when he moved away from the machine to get some milk from the fridge, and then, typically, she heard herself rattling on in an inane manner about, of all things, the wretched coffee maker. Asking him how on earth he could possibly understand something that looked so alien, sounding like a brainless bimbo instead of the qualified professional that she was.

'Really,' she said, in a last-ditch attempt to rescue herself from complete idiocy, 'what I mean is that I really don't understand why anyone would want to bother with something that just takes so much time to do so little.'

'It's an expensive gadget.' He handed her a royal-blue cup filled with some very frothy coffee and then leaned down, resting his elbows on the counter, which was a manoeuvre that brought his disconcertingly close to her. Melissa pulled back and made indistinct yummy noises while her heart began to thud like a drum inside her.

'Men like gadgets and rich men like expensive gadgets. Or so one of my exes thought when she decided to buy this for me as a birthday present. Makes good coffee, though.'

'What…an unusual present to buy your boyfriend,' Melissa mused aloud, her imagination now swerving madly to what sort of women he went out with. There had been no seedy pictures of him leaving clubs with a woman on his arm but now she thought that any woman who gave a man a sophisticated piece of kitchen gadgetry must be as sophisticated as he was. 'Maybe it was a hint that she wanted you to spend more time in the kitchen,' she said, voicing her thoughts. When there was no response, she glanced at him to find that he was watching her coolly. 'Or maybe,' she continued, remembering that she was there in an official capacity and not as some kind of chum free to express her thoughts on any and everything, 'her father owned a kitchen shop and there were a few going spare.' She smiled nervously and sipped some coffee. 'What time does Lucy usually get home?'

Elliot glanced at his watch and frowned. 'A little before four, I believe.'

'You believe?'

'I can't say that I'm generally around to meet her when she gets in from school,' he answered irritably. 'Lenka is normally here, although the child *is* fourteen years old, after all, and fully capable of letting herself into the apartment. That's nothing that a lot of teenagers don't do themselves.'

'I never did,' Melissa said. 'My mum was a great believer in a stable home environment. I would get the bus home from school and she was always there, waiting by the door. Probably a very old-fashioned concept these days. I can't really imagine what it must be like to still be a child and then have to get back to an empty house and start preparing some food for yourself…'

'Can't you?' He strolled over to the fridge, hunted out a plastic container of juice and poured himself a glass. He didn't return to the counter, but instead remained where he was, on the opposite side of the kitchen, half leaning against the imposing American-style fridge. 'I don't really think it takes an unusual amount of imagination to deal with the concept and, unlike you, I don't think accepting some responsibility at the age of fourteen is undesirable.' He didn't like the expression on her face. She had the slightly superior look of someone who thought that whatever they were hearing was really a lot of drivel. It grated. 'In fact,' he said flatly, 'I myself was quite accustomed to doing much the same myself. My parents lived in the Far East and from the age of fourteen I was quite used to spending at least some of the holidays and all of the half-terms in our London flat, often by myself. It never did *me* any harm.' He drank down the juice in one long gulp and dumped the empty glass directly into the sink.

'Didn't you get…lonely?' Melissa asked. She cradled the cup in her hands and stared absentmindedly at the remainder of the coffee, which was now quite tepid. In her head, she was imagining Elliot as a teenager, letting himself into a flat somewhere, laden down with school books and a rucksack full of dirty washing.

'Of course not!' Elliot dismissed scornfully. The conversation was now really beginning to get on his nerves. 'I gained self-reliance and believe me when I tell you that, to get anywhere in life, self-reliance is essential.'

She didn't say anything to that, but she was looking at him now, blonde hair escaping in tendrils around her face and big blue eyes full of disbelief. It took a supreme effort not to pursue the topic until he wiped that disbelief from her face, but then he reminded himself that her thoughts on matters unrelated to what she was going to be paid to do were of no relevance to him whatsoever.

'Yes. Of course.'

Mouthing platitudes, he thought with another huge surge of irritation. Just saying what she expected he wanted to hear because he was, after all, now her employer and a very generous one at that.

'Which brings us back to Lucy. Where the hell is she?'

'Sometimes there are after-school things going on.'

'Sometimes there are,' Elliot grated, 'but not today. I made it perfectly clear to her that she was to be back here promptly by four so that she could meet you.' He pulled out his cellphone, flicked through the directory and scowled at his watch while he waited for whoever he was calling to pick up. When it was picked up, there wasn't much Melissa could glean from the conversation. He barked out a few questions then listened, finally ringing off, only to make a couple more calls. These she could understand. One was to the school, the other to a private number. Both parties confirmed that Lucy had left school on time.

'Where is she?' Melissa asked. 'Did they say?'

'Where she should be,' Elliot said, 'is here. Where she is…' he prowled restlessly, frowning, into the sitting area and Melissa swivelled on the bar stool to follow him '…no one appears to know…'

CHAPTER THREE

IT WAS nearly forty minutes before Lenka arrived at the apartment, flustered and concerned. Melissa was sitting on a sofa and for a few minutes the girl had no awareness that Elliot wasn't alone. In that time, Melissa had the opportunity to watch their interaction.

Lenka, from what she could judge, was no older than eighteen or nineteen, a thin, brown-haired girl with an anxious face, now creased into further lines of worry as she spoke to Elliot in broken English.

And, judging from the poor girl's expression, she was as intimidated by her employer as everyone else on the face of the earth probably was. Melissa could understand why. The minute she walked through the door, Elliot had made no effort to put her at ease. He had towered over her like judge and jury rolled into one, and Melissa could see Lenka visibly flinch as a series of questions were fired out at her. There was nothing accusatory in any of the questions, but he was not a sympathetic inquisitor.

Did the man ever relax? she wondered. And behave like a normal human being?

At the end of five minutes, with her role of spectator becoming increasingly uncomfortable, Melissa pointedly cleared her throat and Lenka immediately swung round to look at her. The relief at seeing another female made her shoulders sag and then she promptly repeated everything she had just told Elliot, wringing her hands with such obvious dismay that Melissa stood up and walked over so that she could give the girl a comforting hug.

'Calm down,' she said, drawing Lenka to the sofa,

'nothing is your fault.' She glanced over her shoulder to see Elliot staring at them with a face still like thunder.

'Perhaps Lenka might like a cup of tea, or coffee?'

Elliot looked at her as though tempted to ask where she was proceeding with that remark. Melissa decided to make it perfectly clear.

'She's distraught,' she said firmly. 'I think a strong cup of tea with some sugar might be a good idea. Would you mind…?'

She realised what it must feel like to ask someone a question that was so utterly incomprehensible that you might as well be talking in another language, and for some reason she felt a sudden rush of heady power. For the first time she had come into contact with him, he was not in a position to assert his stamp of authority and to do precisely what he wanted to do. She was trying to calm down his hysterical housekeeper and, with a question placed so directly, he had no option but to do as she had requested.

He brought the tea over, sat down heavily on the chair facing them and watched as Melissa coaxed some calm into Lenka. It was all a protracted business and one that was bringing them no closer to sorting out the disappearance of his daughter, if disappearance was what it was.

After a few minutes, during which time his impatience went up a few more notches, he said curtly, 'It's now nearly six. Lenka, have you any idea at all where Lucy might be?'

He had to stop himself from obeying his instinct to act by telling the girl to pull herself together. As though reading his mind, Melissa looked across at him warningly.

'Any idea at all, Lenka?' Melissa translated the question into something less blatantly and impatiently aggressive.

Lenka, after fighting the temptation to resume her hysterics, dabbed her red-rimmed eyes with a handkerchief that had been produced seemingly from nowhere, and gave the question some thought.

Lucy, apparently, had no friends, or none that she had ever brought back with her to the apartment. She very rarely stayed at school for any extracurricular activities, apart from sports, which was on a Friday. But even taking that into account, no, she couldn't understand why Lucy would not be home.

'I do not know where she could go!' Lenka looked completely bewildered by the situation.

'What about...' Melissa looked hesitantly over at Elliot '...any boys, Lenka? Has Lucy ever mentioned a boy to you? It's important you tell the truth here—'

'Don't be ridiculous!' Elliot interrupted harshly. 'Boys? The girl is fourteen!'

'Old enough, according to you, to come back here and stay on her own, to develop some essential *self-reliance*. Well, if a girl is old enough to do that then she's old enough to have a boyfriend!' Old enough, she left unsaid, to seek an outlet for her own unhappiness by trying to find a bit of understanding in the arms of a boy. Fuelled by testosterone, a boy would be more than happy to get rid of a girl's unhappiness in the sack.

It wasn't a palatable thought, but if he wanted to be realistic about her non-appearance, then why spare him the details? Much as it made her sick to think of a child of fourteen being sexually active, Melissa knew that it happened.

Lenka, who had only just managed to follow the sharp conversation between the two of them, was shaking her head.

'No boys,' she said at last. 'She never mentioned one to me. No.'

'In which case,' Elliot rose to his feet and snatched the phone from its cradle, 'we get in touch with the police.'

Melissa didn't bother to tell him that a teenager missing for less than two hours was not going to have them rushing out 'Wanted' posters all over London and gearing up a team of fifty strong to go hunting.

She waited until he had replaced the receiver and then listened diplomatically to his colourful invective as he paced the room, cursing an inept police force, gesticulating to emphasise his complete disgust and challenging her to interrupt, to just *dare*.

Although she wasn't in the firing line for this overwhelming tirade, Lenka cowered further into the sofa as though wishing she could somehow push her way through the upholstery and emerge somewhere else, somewhere safer.

Melissa, on the other hand, felt oddly calm.

She waited until he had finished storming around the room like a caged animal and had flopped into the chair, his face dark with fury.

'I have an idea.'

Elliot looked at her and glowered. 'Why would you suggest that she might have got herself tangled up with some boy?'

'Because,' she sighed, 'it was an avenue that had to be explored. Do you have any experience at all of teenagers, Elliot? I mean, prior to Lucy?' This was the first time that unprompted she had called him by his name and just saying it made her stomach curl. She was horribly and acutely aware of the sheer force of his masculinity as he sat there, his blue eyes broodingly angry and focused on her face with such intensity that she could feel her face slowly suffuse with colour.

She almost forgot about Lenka, sniffing beside her on

the sofa, eyes downcast, hands compulsively twisting the
sodden handkerchief.

'What does that have to do with anything?' Elliot
growled.

'I take it that means no. Well, girls these days aren't
quite the shrinking violets they were a few years ago…'

'Whoever said they were shrinking violets *then*?' His
sexy mouth curved into a sudden knowing smile.

'A vulnerable, isolated young girl would be a very easy
target for a boy or even, heaven forbid, a man. But I'm
pretty sure Lucy would have mentioned something to
Lenka.'

At the mention of her name, Lenka looked up and
nodded vigorously.

'She say nothing to me about going out with a boy.
She come home and go to her bedroom and do her homework.'

'I think we should check the cafés close by. She might
just have gone into one of them and forgotten the time.'

Melissa stood up, itching to be out of the grand apartment and the gathering storm clouds. Whatever Lenka
had said, there was still a chance that Lucy had become
involved with someone, possibly someone undesirable,
and heaven help her if she had. She glanced at Elliot's
closed, angry face and shivered.

He turned to Lenka, who automatically cringed back
into the chair, and informed her that she could leave.

'We'll handle the search,' he said, looking round at
Melissa. 'There are enough cafés on Gloucester Road to
keep us busy for hours. Dammit! This is just what I didn't
need. Scouring the streets of London for a runaway
child.'

'We don't know that she's run away,' Melissa said, as
they hit the warm pavement outside.

'No, you're right. Like you said, she might just have

got herself tied up reading a really good book in the park somewhere.'

'I didn't think about the park. Maybe we should check there first.'

'And how do you suggest we do that?' He stopped and looked down at her. 'Maybe find ourselves a couple of loud-hailers and stroll around asking for one miscreant by the name of Lucy to come out of hiding and face the music?'

Melissa met his hard blue eyes steadily. She would love to have told him how dislikeable he was but common sense warned her to hold her tongue. Elliot was not a man to be criticised and she didn't want to find herself dismissed before she had even begun her job.

But he was right. Searching the park was out of the question. It was too big. But they did go there to have a quick look, on the slim off-chance that they might just get lucky and spot Lucy.

On a balmy early-June evening, it was crowded. Groups of people were sitting on the grass, office workers who had discarded their jackets and rolled up their sleeves. Some of the girls had come prepared for the weather and were lying back with their trousers pulled up as far as they possibly could be and bikini tops on, enjoying the warmth. The paths that wound around and through the park were full of people on bicycles and skateboards. There were even a few on horses, which looked bizarre to Melissa, who associated horse riding with country lanes.

It was only just June but already the summer was proving to be a hot one. Melissa found it uncomfortable. She was accustomed to cooler weather and up there in Yorkshire, even on hot days, there was still a breeze that blew across the open land and carried some relief from the stickiness that had built up in the city.

Elliot hadn't changed out of his suit, but he was no longer wearing a jacket and he, too, had rolled back the sleeves of his shirt, exposing his muscular arms dusted with fine, dark hair.

He moved with quick, purposeful strides through the park. He had told her that there was no point trying to scour every inch because it was impractical, but they could look around the area of park closest to the road, where she might have gone to laze around in the sunshine.

No one could have mistaken him for a tourist or an office worker detouring for some free relaxation on his way back home. No one could have confused him for anything but what he was, a man grimly searching for someone, inconvenienced and enraged by the fact that he was having to do it.

Not knowing who to look for, Melissa followed him from behind, watching as he strode a while, stopped, squinted slowly in a semicircle the area directly in front of him, then, finding nothing, moved on to do the same until finally he turned to her, his face hard with suppressed anger.

'This is pointless.' He pulled out his cellphone, dialled and waited for a couple of minutes before ending the call. 'No answer on the home phone, so she's either not back or not picking up.'

'What about her mobile phone?'

'Switched off. I suppose this now brings us to plan B. The cafés. And if that doesn't work, then I'll personally go to the police station and force them to start looking.'

They walked along in silence for a short while, away from the park, over the main road and then down towards Gloucester Road, Melissa barely glancing at the elegant, tall edifices on either side. Some were run-down, several fronted with scaffolding, but others were exquisitely maintained, glamorous dwellings in a glamorous post-code. They walked past them, Elliot still lost in his own thoughts.

'What sort of coffee-shop would you imagine a four-teen-year-old girl might frequent?' He finally broke the silence, although he carried on walking while he spoke, not looking at Melissa.

'Ones where they don't mind someone on their own lingering. You know what I mean.'

'If I knew, I wouldn't have asked.' He sighed heavily and raked his fingers through his hair, then he did turn to her with a crooked smile. 'Great start to your new job, wouldn't you agree? You should have been sitting down with my daughter, having a civilised chat in civilised sur-roundings, and instead you're tramping up and down the highways and byways of London searching for her.'

'I don't mind.' She smiled hesitantly.

'That's very generous-minded of you. Do you think we should believe that there isn't a boy involved, even though Lenka is adamant that there's been nothing along those lines going on?' He pulled her towards him to allow someone to get past and continued to watch her face in-tently. 'I doubt she and Lenka would have had the sort of relationship that encourages confidences.'

'There's no point thinking about that now.' Melissa didn't think it would help for him to know that she ech-oed his own suspicions. 'Let's search the places around here first.' She began moving away and he fell into step with her, although now the silence was broken. For the first time, something human peeped out from behind the steel exterior.

'I expect you think that I had a hand in this,' he said expressionlessly. 'That if I had thrown myself into the role of parenting, I wouldn't now have a daughter who thinks that she has to run away from an insupportable situation.'

'I expect it must have been difficult for you,' Melissa conceded. 'Having a daughter suddenly appear on your doorstep, and a teenager at that. Trying to fit it in with your hectic work schedule… On the other hand,' she continued, compelled to give the full breadth of her views now that she had been asked, so to speak, 'work is nothing compared to family. I mean, did you take *any* time off to get to know her?'

'Of course I did.' Some, he thought, deciding that he had no obligation to justify himself to a complete stranger. 'But teenagers are a fairly uncommunicative species…'

'So you gave up.'

'I gather that work, for you, is a little something that gets done to make way for the bigger issues of having family meals together and singing songs round a piano on winter evenings, but work, for me, is much more than that. It's the driving force that gives meaning to the very act of getting out of bed.'

'Is that why you never married? Never had a family?' Melissa was amazed that she had asked the question, but walking side by side meant that those fabulous, intimidating blue eyes were not on her face, making her squirm inside, scaring her away from the very thought of asking him a personal question. The problem was that asking personal questions was just part of her personality. It was why her clients liked her, why she had been so successful with her charges and with their parents when she had been nannying. She wasn't nosy, she was warmly and vitally interested, although she was surprised why she should be curious about a man for whom she had scant respect, even with his high-powered job, his vast wealth, or, she thought uncomfortably, his incredible looks.

There was something abstracted and only mildly interested in her voice. She wasn't trying to pump confidences out of him, trying to open him up and make him vulnerable, which was the ploy of some of the women he had dated in the past, the ones who thought that they could get past the 'No Entry' sign and somehow turn him into one of those sensitive New Men who were keen to bare their inner souls and were proud of crying.

Melissa was asking a question with no hidden strings attached, and for the first time in as long as he could remember, Elliot didn't automatically go into immediate shut-down.

'Got it in one,' he answered lazily. 'I was smart enough to realise that to have a family and kids would take time, and time was the one thing I didn't have at my disposal.'

'And you…never thought…what it might be like…?'

Elliot laughed, struck by her simplistic view of life. 'No, I really can't say that I ever have. You might think that a teenager is hard to inherit but I'm grateful that I didn't suddenly find myself the father of a toddler. I have no idea what I would have done in that situation.'

'Changed,' Melissa said simply. 'I don't think we need to look in restaurants. I doubt a teenager would be drawn to a restaurant if she wanted to go somewhere to think.'

On either side of the road were two restaurants. If he had wanted to unwind in his own company, he would have gone to either of them. But then, as she had said, what did he know about teenagers? The money angle would not have stopped Lucy from going into whichever damned establishment she chose. He might not have given her his time, but he had been generous with her allowance; overgenerous, some might have said.

'What do you mean *changed*? Changed into what?' Elliot suddenly demanded.

The conversation was punctuated by Elliot stopping so that he could look into some of the shops they walked past. The only way they could cover both sides of the road was by going down one side, turning back on themselves and covering the other, although he had given Melissa a brief description of what Lucy looked like. Approximately five feet seven inches, dark hair, blue eyes, slightly overweight. It could have fitted a thousand girls but she kept her eyes peeled to the other pavement anyway, just in case.

'Changed into someone who had to fit another person into their life, some other responsibility. If you had suddenly found yourself in charge of a toddler, then you wouldn't have had much choice. You might be selfish, but a toddler would have put you to shame.'

'Being selfish is completely different from enjoying what you do for a living.'

'Hmm. I suppose so. Sometimes.'

Well, that was as much a non-answer as he had ever heard, and it got just slightly under his skin, where it was like a burr, rubbing away through the ensuing silence as they continued the search.

It would shortly be getting dark. He tried the phone at the apartment again, and got no reply, then he tried her cellphone and got no joy there either.

It was maddening. Walking up and down like this, stopping in every window so that he could peer in and establish that she was nowhere to be found.

It was also, in a funny kind of way, enjoyable.

He realised that as a form of exercise went, he actually hadn't walked for a very long time. He played squash, he swam, occasionally he used the gym on the ground floor of the apartment block, but walking was something he had come to view as unnecessary and, besides, as with so many things, he simply didn't have the time.

There was more of a purpose to the people hurrying around them now. Some were heading back home, others were starting out for their night's entertainment.

He was about to take her to task for her inaccurate description of him when he stopped suddenly and peered through the window of a coffee-shop. It was busy with an eclectic mix of scruffy youths and smart-looking business people, all perched alongside one another at tables, some staring vacantly into space over their coffee-cups, others talking animatedly in groups.

'She's in there.'

Melissa reached out and held on to his arm. 'Are you sure? Where?'

'Towards the back, reading a book.' His voice was tight with anger.

'Maybe we should just wait a few minutes before we go rushing in.'

Elliot turned around and looked at her coldly. 'Why?'

'Maybe it would be a good idea to calm down a bit...'

'I'm perfectly calm, and let me remind you that you're not being paid to act as amateur psychiatrist. You work at a gym and you've been hired to help with my daughter.'

The human face was gone. The man she disliked was back in full force complete with that withering expression that could make a person feel as small as an ant. But he was right. She worked for him and her place was to do as he said. He might tolerate the occasional flare of rebelliousness, the odd one question too many, but he was an impatient man, accustomed to having his orders obeyed, and when her openness ceased to amuse he would have no qualms in putting her firmly back where she belonged. In her place. In a way, she was surprised that she had been allowed to ask him any personal questions at all, but half his mind would have been engaged in the hunt for his daughter.

'Fine,' Melissa said politely. 'I just thought…'

'Don't. Leave the thinking to me. If I wanted a sparring partner with thoughts and opinions, I would have employed a university lecturer. Got it?'

Elliot didn't give her time to answer, instead swinging round to walk through the glass doors, which had been wedged open to accommodate the fine weather. They had to skirt round the people seated outside and then weave their way through the tables, not one of which was empty. It was a popular café belonging to a chain that was nationwide. Melissa used to go to one very similar to the one right here, when she lived in Yorkshire. Every Saturday she would meet there with her friends because it had a great atmosphere and, although the drinks and coffees were overpriced, they were good and the staff never seemed fussed about moving you on.

Judging from the three mugs in front of her, all with dregs of caramel-coloured liquid at the bottom, this café sported the same easygoing philosophy. Lucy was absorbed in her book and looked as though she had been sitting in the same spot for hours.

In fact, she had no idea that anyone had approached her and Melissa wasn't that surprised. There were so many people in the place, queuing up for drinks, hovering around for a table while staff rushed about busily cleaning vacated surfaces, that she had obviously tuned out the noise factor.

It gave Melissa time to look at the girl in front of her. Long, straight dark hair was loosely tied back into a pony-tail and, although she was definitely plump, her hands were slender, as were her legs, which were tucked under the chair so that she could lean forward to read.

Surprisingly, Elliot hadn't dragged her to her feet so

that he could tear into her, and she was beginning to think that he had maybe come to his senses and realised that understanding was going to be a better way of dealing with the situation than confrontation, when he said softly,

'You'll have an explanation for this, won't you?'

Lucy looked up, not seeing Melissa, just seeing the tall dark man towering over her, and her face blanched.

She was pretty. The long dark hair framed an oval face that had the same vivid blue eyes as her father, and the same expressive mouth. The expression in those blue eyes now went from fear to mulishness.

'I believe you were supposed to return home this afternoon by four? Expressly on my orders?'

'I forgot. Sorry.'

Elliot looked as though he could happily have strangled her, but instead he remained where he was, hands in his pockets, and only the hardening of his jaw betraying his rage. Rage that he had spent hours involved in a frantic search, rage that he had phoned the police station and rage that at the end of all of that her carelessly tossed-out *sorry* was the only thing she was offering by way of an apology.

'*Sorry?* Is that all you have to say?'

Lucy shrugged. It was one of those teenage gestures redolent of insolence and guaranteed to make an enraged adult even more enraged. Melissa felt her lips twitch with an inappropriate smile. For the most part she had been a conformist adolescent, but she could still remember the odd occasion when a gesture very much like the one Lucy had just made was enough to make her parents hopping mad. It was the biggest trump card for the teenager who wanted to be rude without saying a word.

And it was working beautifully.

'Right, miss,' Elliot said through gritted teeth. 'Home.'

'Home? I'd need an airplane to take me there.'

The silence that greeted this remark was shot through with tension, at which point Melissa decided to intervene. She smiled warmly, ignoring Elliot, and held out her hand.

'I'm Melissa.'

Lucy's eyes swept over her, dismissive and sullen. 'Oh, yeah. The keep-fit person he thinks will get rid of my fat.' She didn't take the outstretched hand, nor did she stand up, although the book had fallen shut. 'Bad enough being stuck with a daughter, never mind one who's so unsightly she can't be paraded in public.'

'This isn't the place to be having this conversation,' Elliot said tightly. 'Pick up your schoolbag. We're leaving.'

For a few seconds, Melissa thought that Lucy intended to do no such thing, but then she stuck the book in her rucksack and stood up, taller than Melissa by several inches in her school shoes.

Caught between Elliot, who was striding out of the coffee-shop with a face like thunder, and Lucy, who was dragging her steps behind him like someone on the way to meet a firing squad, Melissa finally opted for Lucy. She fell into step with her and began asking her a few questions about her school, the least provocative line of questioning she could come up with. Answers were either monosyllabic or non-existent, and after a few minutes she fell into an uneasy silence as she eyed the man in front of them.

'He was worried,' she finally said to Lucy, who turned to her for a few seconds before giving a short, bitter laugh.

'Worried? I don't think so. Not in the way you mean. He was annoyed because I was being inconvenient and he doesn't like anyone or anything to inconvenience him.'

That was the longest sentence she had spoken. Her voice was soft, with a pleasing Australian accent.

'People can sometimes get set in their ways,' Melissa offered placatingly. 'And the older they get, the more set they can become.'

She had meant it as an excuse, but Lucy caught on to the concept with spiteful delight. She gave a laugh that caught in her throat and nodded vigorously. 'An old man set in his ways.'

'Well, maybe not *that* old…'

'I don't know what my mum could ever have seen in him. I don't know why she ever went out with him in the first place. If she had never gone out with him…she must have been mad, or stupid or…or…' Unable to get hold of suitable vocabulary to register her emotions, Lucy fell back into silence and Melissa didn't consider it the right time to break it.

They walked on, staring ahead. Elliot obviously assumed that they would be obediently following in his wake because not once did he turn around to make sure that they were still there. He was as consumed in his thoughts as his daughter was.

As soon as they reached the block of apartments, Melissa said as cheerfully as she could under the circumstances that it might be best if she left.

'To try and sort things out…between yourselves…' she finished lamely, when her suggestion was met with deafening silence. Lucy's body language was telling her that she could go or she could stay, it wouldn't matter to her, but there was something of a plea in her eyes that made Melissa feel guilty. Then she wondered why she was feeling guilty when this particular drama had nothing to do with her.

Elliot was more forthcoming. He told her bluntly that she still had work to do, that he would appreciate her trying to put aside the hitch to proceedings and carry on as normal.

'Carry on as normal?' Melissa parroted incredulously.

'That's right. I can order some food in for us to eat.'

Neither he nor his daughter were looking at one another and Melissa was struck by the awkward feeling of being the piggy in the middle.

How had she ever got herself talked into this bizarre arrangement? She had no place being here and being an unwilling audience to words that she would be better off not hearing. She would intervene. She knew she would. And then she would become embroiled in their saga when she didn't want to be.

'I'll just stay to leave the stuff I brought with me…' she stammered, fishing into her capacious handbag. 'I can't stay for anything to eat because…because I have a date…'

'A date?' Elliot frowned. 'You told me you were unattached.'

'Oh, dear,' Lucy said with dripping sarcasm. 'What a nerve, having a private life when it doesn't suit him!'

'I'll get to you in a minute, Lucy.' Elliot swung round to look at her through narrowed eyes.

They had taken the lift up and he unlocked the apartment door, entering first with Lucy scuttling in behind him and Melissa trailing uncomfortably in the background with her pamphlets and book clutched in one hand.

'I'll just leave these things here…' she said, hovering by the door. If she could have managed it, she would have flung them on the nearest counter surface and raced out of the apartment as fast as her legs would take her.

'There's no need,' Lucy said, not looking at her, but staring at her father with hostility. 'I don't need anyone babysitting me!'

'If you're childish enough to think that running away
sorts things out, then—'

'I was *not running away*!' Two patches of angry colour
had appeared on her cheeks. She had dropped her rucksack on the ground and was glaring at her father with
loathing, hands squarely placed on her hips. He, in turn,
was looking at her coldly, a man on the brink of losing
it completely. Melissa seriously considered sneaking out
of the door and making a break for it, but, coward that
she was, she remained rooted to the spot.

'No?'

'No! Where would I run to? I didn't feel like coming
back here to sit and listen to someone give me a lecture
about losing weight so I decided to stop off at a coffee-
shop and read instead! So what? Big deal! Maybe you'll
see that you can't force me to *do anything*!'

'I'm not forcing you to do anything, but while you're
in this house—'

'Oh, please! I'm sick of that stupid argument. It's not
my fault that I'm stuck here with you! Do you
think…that…that…?' She turned away and flopped
down on the sofa, biting back the tears of rage and frustration.

'I apologise for you having to witness this show of
behaviour,' Elliot said, turning to Melissa with eyes like
ice.

'Why apologise?' Lucy looked at Melissa stormily. 'In
case you haven't found out yet, he doesn't apologise for
anything! Ever! *I* should be apologising to you!' She
looked at her father and Melissa could see her face so
close to crumpling that her heart went out to her. 'Apologising for ruining your cosy life with your work…and
your meetings…and your *bloody, bloody* fiancée!'

CHAPTER FOUR

'YOU don't have to do any exercise if you don't want to, you know. I mean, I can't force you. On the other hand, I *am* being paid to at least try and encourage…' Melissa had already given up on anything like vigorous exercise. She had come to the apartment at four-thirty, been confronted by a teenager who would barely speak to her and she was getting very frustrated.

Lucy, probably under orders to be obliging, was making sure that she did exactly the opposite. Right now she was sitting on the sofa with a can of soda in one hand and the remote control in the other, while she flicked from one music channel on the television to another.

'What are the school lunches like?'

No answer.

'What do you have for breakfast?' She was realising that she could actually ask any number of dietary questions until the cows came home and she would get zero response. Lucy wasn't listening. With sudden inspiration, she realised that there was probably only one topic that might encourage her stubborn charge to talk, and so she tacked on, innocently, 'I expect that, since your father wants to encourage you to eat healthily, he sends you off with toast and scrambled egg? Or maybe a bowl of cereal and some fruit…?'

'He's not my father. Don't call him my father. My father was killed in a road accident six months ago.'

Bingo.

'Oh. OK.' Melissa closed the book on her lap, a teenager's guide to healthy eating which she had rummaged

up from the stock of reference books she kept in a suit-
case under her bed. 'What do *you* call him, then?'

'I don't call him anything. In fact, I try not to talk to
him at all.'

'I can't hear you with that music in the background.
What did you say?'

Lucy switched off the television with an elaborate sigh
and turned to face Melissa. 'I *said* that I just don't talk
to him.'

'You must talk *sometimes*.'

'Why? He has nothing to say to me that I want to hear
and vice versa. Anyway, he's hardly ever here.'

'We could talk about this outside,' Melissa suggested
coaxingly. 'Go for a walk in the park...'

'Oh, yeah, I forgot. You're here to babysit me and
make sure I get rid of all this disgusting fat.' The bored
voice was back and Melissa sighed inwardly. It was going to be an uphill struggle every inch of the way, and
the unfortunate circumstances of their meeting weren't
going to make things easier. She hadn't a clue what had
been said between father and daughter the night before,
but she would have bet her last pound that it hadn't been
a pleasant confrontation. After the revelation about his
fiancée, she had managed to sneak away, leaving them
facing one another across the living room like adversaries
about to do battle with one another. And, as expected,
Elliot had been nowhere around when she had arrived
earlier. Nor had Lenka.

'OK, to be blunt, I am supposed to be doing a job,
although I'm beginning to wonder what it is considering
you seem just fine to me.' A tiny white lie never went
amiss, Melissa thought, crossing her fingers behind her
back. The truth was that Lucy was comfort eating, which
wasn't good, and the more the pounds rolled on the lower
her self-esteem would get, and the more her desire for

comfort food would increase. She was at the edge of a vicious circle.

'There's no need to lie. I know I've put on a lot of weight. Nearly two stone since I came over here, but...'

'And if your father thinks that I've been shirking my duties,' Melissa said with a straight face, 'he might just kill me. He can be a very scary man...'

'Tell me about it.' This was spoken with sincerity as Lucy stood up, stretched, looked at her garb, which was some baggy hipster jogging pants and a T-shirt with an obscure band plastered across the front. 'Well, I guess we *could* go out, but I'm not jogging or running or anything.'

'Oh, good. I hate that stuff.'

By the time they were in the park, Melissa felt that some progress was being made. This progress depended on her not mentioning anything about diets, healthy eating or the benefits of an active life, but instead asking questions about Elliot, allowing Lucy to give full vent to her dislike.

After fifteen minutes of strolling, they had covered most of Elliot's more noticeable faults, and Melissa couldn't disagree with any of the findings. He was cold, arrogant, insensitive and impatient of anyone who did not meet his standards.

'I expect that's what comes of devoting so much time to your work,' Melissa felt obliged to contribute, although it was a half-hearted attempt to be unbiased, because, when she thought of the expression on his face when he'd seen his daughter in that coffee-shop, she found herself agreeing with everything Lucy had said.

After half an hour, Lucy had opened up sufficiently to talk about school and what she hated there. This seemed to include everything from the school lunches to the schoolchildren.

But at least she was talking, even though the conversation was almost entirely negative.

'But he's going to send me away to boarding-school anyway.'

Lucy informed Melissa of this as they were heading back to the apartment. The leisurely stroll had at least extended to a brisk walk. Lucy hadn't noticed. She had been too wrapped up in her litany of complaints. Underneath every complaint was a comparison to what she had enjoyed in Australia, although she had not mentioned that part of her life at all. Melissa could feel it simmering unhappily under the surface and she knew better than to try and prompt any discussion of it. When Lucy was ready, she would discuss her past if she chose to.

'Don't be silly. Of course he won't!'

Lucy's reply was scathing. 'I overheard them. That awful woman said that it made sense, that there was no way he could pretend to play happy families, that he'd been landed with me and it would be best for everyone concerned if I boarded, that it would do me good.'

'That awful woman…?'

'His fiancée. Alison Thomas-Brown.' Lucy made a face. 'She's a witch.'

In the interests of being impartial and adult, Melissa scrabbled around to find something to say that was soothing. Of course Elliot wouldn't have become engaged to someone unpleasant enough to be called a witch, although to a displaced teenager that might well be the description that came to mind when her one slice of fragile security was being threatened. Lucy might not have found herself the cosy, welcoming father she had hoped for, but he was still her father, still her one certainty in her suddenly fractured life. In other words, underneath all the bluster and antipathy, he was still better than nothing.

They had reached the apartment block. The porters knew Lucy very well by now and Melissa's gardening book was waiting for her, courtesy of the porter with the interest in plants. They chatted for a while about plants, then about his daughters, who were both at university, and about his wife, who worked as a cleaner in one of the hospitals. Eventually Lucy cleared her throat and Melissa broke off their chat to smile at her.

'I know,' Melissa whispered sheepishly as they took the elevator up. 'I can't help it. I just find people so interesting; there's always something going on in their lives even though you'd never guess it to look at them.'

'There's nothing going on in my life,' Lucy said sadly. 'There used to be but now…'

'Would you like to go to a movie with me tomorrow?' Melissa asked, on the spur of the moment. 'I know it's a weekday but perhaps your father would let you just this once. There's a great Disney film showing…'

Without realising it, Melissa had hit on a shared love that lit up Lucy's face. The permanent sullenness vanished and the first true shy smile peeped out.

So Melissa was feeling rather successful on day two by the time they made it up to the apartment, where Elliot was waiting for them.

Neither of them was expecting him. Wasn't he the man who only had time for work? The man who found it nigh on impossible to tear himself away from the seductive allure of the office? What was he doing back at…Melissa surreptitiously looked at her watch…at six thirty-five? And in casual clothes, which implied that he had been back at the apartment even earlier?

He was sitting on the sprawling sofa, with a glass of white wine in one hand, and he had been reading the

Financial Times, which he lowered as soon as they walked in. On the table in front of him was his open laptop computer.

Warm, sticky and fairly sweaty after twenty minutes of brisk walking, Melissa was suddenly and acutely conscious of her appearance. She had dressed in leggings, trainers and a short-sleeved white T-shirt that was far more fitted than the usual baggy tops she normally favoured. Practical gear but now woefully unflattering as she stood here, being appraised by her elegant, dangerously sexy, good-looking employer.

'Where have you two been? Had a good time?'

Lucy flounced into the kitchen, opened the fridge, took out a block of cheese, then she caught Melissa's eye and put it back. 'What are you doing here?' she asked ungraciously. 'Did you come back to check and make sure that I hadn't run away again?'

Elliot's mouth thinned. 'I wanted to see how your first day with Melissa went. I'm not asking for anything too elaborate but a civil response might be nice.'

Lucy reddened. 'We went for a walk.'

'It's absolutely beautiful out there.' Melissa decided that a rescue operation was called for. How was it possible for tension levels to rise within such a short space of time? The minute Lucy had walked through the door and seen her father, a shutter had dropped over her eyes. And she had immediately reached for some comfort food. 'Makes you want to be outside.' She tentatively approached Elliot, ready to account for her time but guiltily aware that strolls in the sunshine weren't perhaps quite what he had had in mind when he had originally employed her. Aggressive sprinting, maybe. Followed by a dinner of carrot juice and wafer thins.

'You never said why you were home at this hour.' Lucy stood in front of him with her arms folded. 'Home early two days in a row! Isn't the company going to have some kind of nervous breakdown without you at the helm running it?'

Elliot's lips twitched. 'I think they just might be able to cope with my absences, although I can't promise anything if I decide to have another day home early. The paramedics might just have to be called in.'

Not knowing whether he was joking or not, Lucy remained frowning. 'Well, I've got homework to do,' she muttered eventually.

'What about some dinner first?' he asked. 'Lenka usually sees about Lucy's evening meal but she's got some kind of cold.' He turned to Melissa, who looked at him innocently.

'And I guess you've prepared something?' Melissa enquired.

Lucy, who had been heading towards her bedroom, paused and looked over her shoulder with a smirk, tempted to watch him wriggle out of that but eventually deciding that she just couldn't be bothered to show any interest.

'Does it look as though I have?' Elliot asked politely.

'Oh, yes, I forgot. Teenagers are fully capable of looking after themselves.' And yes, at the age of fourteen, Lucy probably could knock up something halfway respectable in the high-tech kitchen. But still… 'I really should be heading home now if there's nothing left for me to do…'

Elliot shoved the newspaper off his lap and extended his long legs on the coffee-table in front of him. Then he linked his fingers behind his head and leaned back to give her the full benefit of that look, that disconcerting, intrusive gaze that made her stomach twist into knots.

'The reason I came home early was that we could have a talk,' he informed her, 'before I go out.'

'It's too early to be making progress with…with Lucy's weight,' Melissa replied faintly. Of course she now had to stay, which meant that she would have to sit down instead of hovering, and that was something she was becoming adept at whenever she was in the man's presence. An idea struck her. 'I could cook something for her to eat,' she suggested, 'unless you'd rather question me here…?'

Elliot suppressed a sigh of pure annoyance. 'I wasn't planning on *questioning* you,' he said levelly. 'I thought we might have a chat, to find out your impressions.' He stood up in one swift, fluid movement, which had her taking a few awkward steps back. 'The cooking idea sounds good.'

It had. Until it occurred to Melissa that running around in his kitchen, making herself at home, would involve her being under the microscope even more than if she had just kept her mouth shut, answered his questions and then left.

Too late. He was heading towards the kitchen and she trailed along behind him.

'Lenka does the shopping,' he said, pulling open one of the cupboards and then staring inside as though the contents were as much a revelation to him as they would be to her. 'Feel free to use whatever you want.'

He pulled out a stool, sat down and proceeded to watch as she rustled in the salad compartment of the fridge, extracted ingredients for something very quick and very simple and then, after a couple of aborted attempts, found the utensils she needed.

She could feel him watching her. 'You could help,' she said at last. 'Chop this.' She handed him a knife, a board and an onion. 'You do know how to chop, don't you?'

'I think I could manage. Tell me how your afternoon

went. I came home because I thought that Lucy might just refuse to be compliant.' He was meticulously peeling off the outer skin. 'Why did you give me the onion?' he asked. 'It's damned fiddly.' He began chopping. 'And it's making my eyes water.'

'Surely you've cried before,' Melissa said, grinning, and he raised his eyebrows.

'Not that I can remember.'

'Because real men don't cry?'

'And quite a few don't chop onions either. What did the two of you talk about?'

'Stuff.' She had efficiently disposed of the mushrooms, the red pepper and the courgette. 'Teenage angst.' After a few seconds of thought, she went to stand where he was still struggling with the onion.

'Have you come to dry my eyes?' he drawled. 'Kiss my tears better?'

Melissa's mouth dropped slightly open and she blushed. Here was a woman not used to flirting, Elliot thought drily, and it was unfair to embarrass her, but it was still gratifying to see her go pink like that. He had never met a woman who blushed as easily as she did. She looked as though she literally couldn't find it in herself to speak.

'I wasn't being serious,' Elliot said gravely.

'I realise that!'

'I don't suppose very many of your clients flirt with you...'

'Most of my clients are of the female variety and no, they don't flirt. I really think that that sort of thing isn't appropriate, given our circumstances...'

'Our circumstances?'

Was he laughing at her? 'I work for you,' Melissa elaborated uncomfortably.

'True.' He sounded suitably in agreement but now, for

some reason, there was a devil inside him. This was a devil that rarely made an appearance. In fact, he couldn't think offhand when the last time was that he had found such enjoyment in stringing out a situation, and he found himself delighting in the delicate bloom of Melissa's cheeks as she fought against her discomfiture.

'Oh, yes, of course you do. And I genuinely didn't want to make you uncomfortable, although…' he paused, pressed his thumbs against his eyes and then looked straight at her '…flirting is only dangerous if it gets out of hand.'

'Gets out of hand…?' Melissa repeated nervously.

'Of course. You're experienced enough to realise that, I'm sure. Any flirting that leads beyond the bedroom door is dangerous…'

'I wasn't suggesting…!' Melissa burst out, horrified. Had he been thinking that she might take him seriously? Think that he was making a pass at her? She thought of him leading her to that dangerous place beyond the bedroom door, and her cheeks burnt.

'I realise that.' Elliot also realised that he had a fiancée, one he was due to see in under an hour, and that amusing himself at the expense of a shy, inexperienced young woman was inexcusable. Efficient she might well be at her job, but he had known enough women in his lifetime to recognise one who was still green around the ears. Moreover he never mixed business with pleasure. 'Onions chopped. Anything else?'

'No. What I'm cooking is a vegetable pasta dish. It's very healthy, very nutritious and it's filling. I think the main thing should be to get Lucy eating healthily and her metabolism will do the rest. I've noticed that she has a tendency to perhaps resort to junk food when she feels under pressure. We all do it, but it's a habit that can be easily stopped.'

Elliot listened in silence as Melissa chattered with her back to him, busying herself with the process of frying ingredients in a pan. His first impression of her had been of someone small and shapeless. She wasn't. Or rather, she wasn't shapeless. Far from it. His eyes wandered lazily over her, taking in the curves that were so unfashionable nowadays. She half turned and reached up to fetch the pasta from the top cupboard. Her breasts, he thought, were surprisingly large for someone not particularly tall. Was that why she wore such unflattering clothes? Because she wanted to cover them up? Even her T-shirt was prudish, with its high round neckline, the sort of T-shirt that made damn sure that not one extra inch of skin was exposed than was absolutely necessary.

'You'll have to go into all this diet stuff with Lenka,' he said, more sharply than he had meant, because he hadn't cared for the road his imagination had decided to go down. Or the ache in his groin it had caused.

'Because you're not interested?' Melissa turned towards him and folded her arms. His sudden change of tone had her immediately on the defensive. Maybe he had clocked that she had actually rather enjoyed that light banter for a while, and this was his way of reminding her of her position. It wasn't as his conversational equal. She was there to impart information.

'Naturally I'm interested, but, as I've already said, I lack the time to put all your helpful culinary hints into practice.'

'Lucy's miserable over here. I gather she feels that she can't talk to you…'

'Of course she can talk to me!' he snapped.

'What about?'

'What do you mean, *what about*?'

'She's lonely and confused. I don't think she feels at home here.'

'It'll take time. What are your plans for tomorrow?'

Melissa guiltily wondered how going to a movie with his daughter could be construed as helpful exercise, which was what she was being paid for. 'I need to get to know Lucy before I can start preaching to her about what to eat and how to exercise. It's a little different from working in a gym.' She went to stand in front of him and leaned against the counter. At least with him sitting on the stool, she was more or less on eye level with him. 'When people come to a gym it's because they want to be there, and they want to be put through their paces. I don't suppose Lucy wants me around and she probably thinks that it's an insult that she's being made to exercise.'

'Why would she think that it's an insult?'

'Wouldn't you?' she asked, without bothering to beat about the bush. 'If someone signed you up to start lifting weights, what would you think?'

'I would be quite flattered that they cared enough to go through the trouble.'

'You're deliberately being obtuse.'

And she was getting all hot under the collar. 'I get the point,' he said eventually. 'But you still haven't told me your plans for tomorrow.'

'What are *yours*?' Melissa threw the question neatly back at him, catching him on the back foot. 'It's not good enough for you to shift your responsibilities onto my shoulders. You have to have some input as well!'

'Shift my responsibilities?'

Melissa chose to ignore the soft menace behind the question. 'I'm going to take Lucy to see a movie tomorrow if that's all right with you, and I think you ought to come along.'

'You're going to a movie?'

'I need to gain her confidence. And I think it might be a good idea if you came too.'

'You mean just drop everything I have on at the moment so that I can go to the cinema.'

Melissa drew in her breath and refused to feel like the naïve moron his tone of voice had implied.

'That's about the size of it.'

'Amazing,' he said, shaking his head the way someone did when confronted by a spectacularly thick child. 'Nothing's sunk in there, has it?'

'What do you mean?' Melissa turned away to go and switch off the hob.

'I can't just take time off work whenever I choose to go to the movies. That's not how business operates.'

'I think it would be nice for Lucy.' The man was from a different planet. Yes, sometimes he seemed human enough, but most of the time he was an alien.

The silence stretched on for so long that she was about to drop the subject completely when she saw him nod imperceptibly.

'OK. I'll come.'

'You'll come?' Melissa heard herself ask incredulously. 'But what about all that work that can't possibly be left? What about the world of business and how it operates?'

'Getting cold feet now that you've got what you wanted?' Elliot drawled silkily. He would have to cancel a few meetings, but what the hell? He and Lucy seemed to have reached a point of total communication meltdown. A movie, with Melissa there as a third party to help dilute the inevitable tension, was a good idea. And besides... He looked at Melissa through half-closed lids and held back the thought.

'Not at all! But if you come, you have to promise that

you won't moan about the work you're missing. There's nothing worse than someone constantly reminding you that they're doing you a favour.'

'Have you ever considered a career in the prison service?' He was beginning to enjoy the way she blushed at the slightest remark. Like now. Except this time she turned away and began filling a saucepan with water for the pasta. 'It was a piece of sarcasm, Melissa, not a personal insult.'

'I know that!'

'You'll have to toughen up in this city, you know.' He looked at her as she buried her thoughts in the pretence of being busy.

'Toughen up?' Melissa repeated vaguely.

'Not let other people affect you quite so much.'

'You don't *affect* me!'

'Because,' Elliot continued, overriding her denial with an expertise born from experience, 'London is full of predators and an innocent like you could end up getting badly hurt.'

Melissa wondered how the conversation had managed to come round to the mortifying place that it had. She wondered whether he had started thinking about her overreaction to his passing, unthinking, flirtatious one-liner. Did he think that he was suddenly responsible for her because she happened to be working for him?

'Thank you for that. I think I can deal with predators.'

'Can you? Have you had much experience of them? In...Yorkshire?'

'Yes, I do happen to know that there are people out there who will take advantage of someone else, but I'm not the country hick you seem to think I am.'

If he had carried on the conversation, it wouldn't have been so bad—at least then she might have had the opportunity to win her case that she wasn't the complete simpleton he thought she was—but he didn't. He just looked at her steadily and speculatively for a few seconds, then asked her which cinema they intended to go to and what time the film started.

'I'll head home as soon as I've cooked this…'

'No need to rush. You can stay and share dinner with Lucy. I won't be around.' He glanced at his watch and stood up, stretching.

'Are you going anywhere nice?' Melissa asked politely.

'A very expensive restaurant in Sloane Square. Would you consider that nice?'

'I suppose it depends who you go with,' Melissa said immediately. 'I guess you're going with your fiancée, so I'm sure it'll be lovely, just as anywhere would be lovely when you're with someone you're in love with.'

'You're really going to have to do something about your naïveté if you're to survive in London,' Elliot commented wryly. He sauntered towards Lucy's bedroom and Melissa could hear him knocking on the door and, when it wasn't opened, saying goodbye to it.

Melissa was beginning to get the picture of what he thought about her. She was inexperienced and simple and when he wasn't laying down laws around her and treating her like something unfortunate he had happened to bump into, he was patronising her.

She was on the verge of telling him just what she thought of *him* when the doorbell rang and Elliot went to answer it without sparing a glance in her direction.

From where she was, wiping down the kitchen counter, she had a bird's-eye view of him as he pulled open the door, could see the slow smile tilt the corners of his mouth, softening the harshness of his face into an expression of devastating charm.

Melissa felt her heart skip a beat. Then she heard a husky laugh and he stepped back to let Alison in.

He was still smiling as he brought her over and introduced her. Alison Thomas-Brown, his fiancée, a barrister in chambers. Melissa had never felt as undersized, underdressed and under-prepared as she felt now. This woman took sophistication into another dimension. She was tall, wafer-thin, with straight black hair and dark eyes that radiated intelligence. Melissa had to look up at her and the hand that briefly shook hers was cool and beautifully manicured.

'Elliot told me about you,' she said politely. 'I do hope you make headway with Lucy. It's been rather dreadful for poor Elliot being stuck with a surly teenager he can't handle.' She turned to Elliot and smiled. 'Although everyone needs one unmanageable situation in their life at some point.'

'I fail to see why,' Elliot replied.

'Most people have more than just one unmanageable situation crop up in their life,' Melissa added truthfully. 'Actually, a lot of people have unmanageable situations crop up virtually on a daily basis!'

Alison laughed politely and Elliot disappeared, saying that he had to get his mobile phone from the bedroom.

Which left Melissa staring up at Alison and wondering what to say next. She was beautiful, she was intelligent, but warm she certainly wasn't.

'I dare say you've already noticed how absolutely impossible it is for Elliot to tailor his lifestyle around Lucy. It smells awfully good in here. Have you cooked?'

'I wouldn't say *impossible*...'

Alison had taken a few steps into the kitchen and was now lifting the lid of the saucepan and inspecting the simmering sauce. 'You clever little thing,' she said appreciatively. 'I can see that Lucy will absolutely thrive in your company!' Her dark eyes hardened fractionally. She glanced quickly in the direction of the bedrooms. 'Poor child. I feel for her, I really do, but I hope you'll agree that we must all be practical about this. Lucy needs people with her and Elliot and myself simply cannot fit our hectic working lives around that bald fact. I've suggested to Elliot that perhaps a boarding-school might be worth thinking about.'

'I don't think—'

'You're not paid to think,' Alison said flatly. 'You're paid to try and get the child into shape so that she can feel a bit more self-confident. Body image is a crucial part of a young girl's sense of self-esteem.'

'Yes, that's true enough but—'

'Call me a fool, but in my profession hard facts speak for themselves. I do suggest you try and warm Lucy to the idea of boarding. I'm sure a talented girl like yourself wouldn't find that an impossible feat?'

Melissa couldn't imagine anyone having the nerve to call Alison Thomas-Brown a fool. They wouldn't dare. She looked as though she might have ways of making her critics suffer and some of them would hurt.

'It's not up to me to try and persuade Lucy to think anything. I'm not an intermediary. Like you said, I'm just here to do a job.'

Alison didn't answer. She had removed herself from the saucepan of food. Just in case some of the sauce spilled accidentally on her designer outfit, Melissa imagined. Now she looked at Melissa thoughtfully.

'But you'll be seeing a lot of Lucy,' Alison said in a low, calm voice, the sort of voice that brooked no argument. 'And sooner or later Lucy will begin chatting. I've tried to draw her out of her shell, but she's been hellishly uncommunicative. You, on the other hand, are probably far more on her level than I, and so will undoubtedly have more success on that front... Elliot will take your cooperation for granted. He is, after all, your employer.'

Melissa, still wrestling with the implied insult that she was on the same wavelength as a fourteen-year-old child, took a few seconds to register the hint of a threat in the latter part of Alison's speech. Before she could open her mouth to protest, Alison continued in her mellifluous voice,

'And for your own protection, I suggest you be careful with Elliot. He can be a charismatic man. I don't think even he is aware of just how attractive that can be to a woman.' She laughed huskily and gave Melissa one of those girlish you-know-what-I-mean looks that was supposed to draw her into the little confidential circle.

'I haven't noticed,' Melissa said, pulling back and hoping that either Lucy or Elliot would emerge from wherever they had inconveniently hidden themselves.

'Oh. Well, maybe it's your tender age. I suppose you're into young lads, boys more your own age?'

Melissa was spared the ordeal of finding a suitable answer to this by the appearance of both Lucy and Elliot at the same time, coming from different directions. When you're looking for a bus, she thought...

She glanced at Elliot and yes, she could see that he might be considered charismatic.

What Alison had forgotten, even with that sharp brain of hers, was that charisma only worked when it was applied and Elliot had absolutely none to spare for an employee. And even if he had, Melissa thought, watching as he bent to murmur something into Alison's ear before turning to Lucy and exchanging their usual monosyllables, she would still be immune.

Good looks and money might work wonders with most women, but when everything else was missing, then, as far as Melissa was concerned, both were about as useful as a box of matches in a fire.

CHAPTER FIVE

THE movie was showing at a small cinema on the King's Road that looked as though it had been lifted out of another century. At first, Lucy was appalled at the size of it but after five minutes she had come round to saying that she supposed it was quite sweet.

'I've never been to a cinema that had a real bar in it,' she commented, scanning the room and sipping her diet soda. 'He's cute.'

'You need to come up to Yorkshire,' Melissa said, smiling; 'where I grew up, there's still the original cinema, and if you think this looks old-fashioned you need to see the one where we still go in my village. Maybe cute isn't quite the right word though...' She grinned. 'Maybe downright uncomfortable. There's still someone who comes round selling ice creams before the movie starts. She looks about a hundred.'

So far Melissa had managed to avoid telling Lucy that her father would be coming to the movies with them. She feared the inevitable outburst and, besides, she was fairly sure that Elliot wouldn't turn up and, however much Lucy professed to loathe him, she would still be disappointed if he didn't appear.

But Melissa's eyes kept skittering towards the door, and her nerves were on edge.

'What did my father say when you told him that we were going to be spending day three at the cinema?' Lucy asked with a little sneer in her voice. 'Did he hit the roof? Bet he did. He wouldn't be able to stand the thought of you not actually having got me going on a treadmill as yet. Ha, ha. He probably thought that by now I would have shed bucket-loads of weight, and then I could become a happy, normal teenager and he could forget about me without a guilty conscience!'

'We'll have to get around to some dietary facts and exercise soon,' Melissa said evasively. Every three seconds, she glanced towards the door, expecting to see Elliot's tall, muscular frame outlined in the doorway, but there was still no sign of him. Perhaps he had mentioned it to Alison and she had decided to ban him from coming.

The little woman-to-woman chat Melissa had endured had stayed with her for the day. She wasn't normally the sort of person who dwelled on unhappy thoughts, but Alison's warnings had hit home. She had chewed over the suggestion-cum-order that she do as she was told and recommend the bliss of boarding with Lucy even if she didn't agree with the concept, and she had fretted over the insinuation that she was somehow inferior. Overriding both of those niggles was Alison's mortifying warning that she should make sure to have as little to do with Elliot as possible just in case she lost her senses and fell for his so-called charisma.

She hadn't even had the opportunity to defend herself! No wonder the woman was a barrister. Melissa felt heartily sorry for anyone confronted with a cross-examination by her. Even if they hadn't committed the crime, they would have been inclined to confess through fear.

Her eyes had gone blank as she replayed the conversation in her head. When they refocused she saw him, just as she had pictured, standing in the doorway, looking around, eyes sharp.

He had come straight from work. That much was obvious from the suit, although he was carrying his jacket slung over one shoulder. Their eyes met and something curled inside her stomach before she looked away hurriedly.

Must be his dashing charisma, she told herself sarcastically, positively exuding from lips that seldom smiled and eyes that could freeze blood.

Melissa had just enough time to interrupt what Lucy was saying and exclaim that her father had just arrived.

The surprise momentarily deprived Lucy of speech and her mouth was still half opened by the time her father had closed the space between them and taken a chair at their table.

'I take it Melissa didn't remember to tell you that I might be coming along this afternoon?' He looked at Lucy, eyebrows raised. 'Close your mouth—you'll catch flies.'

Lucy abruptly closed her mouth and Melissa could see her grappling to find a truly horrendous dig, but just seeing him there had done something to her vocal cords.

'I wasn't sure whether you would be able to make it,' Melissa said coolly, 'and I didn't think it would be fair to get Lucy's hopes raised only to be dashed if you failed to appear.'

'Get my hopes raised? I don't think so!' Lucy scoffed.

'Thank you, Lucy. That makes me feel truly welcome.'

'Well, what can you expect? You haven't been around for the past six months!'

'I'm around now.'

'Why?'

Elliot sighed wearily and glanced across to where Melissa was sitting nervously cradling her cappuccino. 'Although,' he continued, looking at her, 'I glanced at the board outside and there's nothing showing under fifteen.'

'Oh, please!' Lucy interrupted. 'I've been going to fifteen-certificate movies for over a year! I *do* happen to know about sex and bad language!' She flushed and scowled to cover her embarrassment.

'Actually,' Melissa said, rescuing her, 'we're going to see the Disney movie.'

Elliot looked at them. It was on the tip of his tongue to make the obvious remark, that taking valuable time off work was bad enough, but to take it off in order to watch a cartoon was unthinkable. Then it occurred to him that he didn't mind being here. He had had very little time for his daughter since she had moved in with him; in fact had avoided her whenever possible because he had no idea how to connect with her. Being here was good. He looked at the amused grin tugging the corner of Melissa's mouth and felt a dangerous kick of excitement which he kept to himself, surveying her blandly with hooded eyes.

'Don't tell me,' she said, 'you've suddenly remembered an appointment you have to keep.'

She and Lucy exchanged a quick look which Elliot didn't miss.

'Are you two ganging up on me?' he drawled.

'When was the last time you went to see a Disney movie?' Lucy shot at him, always ready to wage war, although her tone wasn't quite as belligerent as it usually was. 'I bet you've never seen one in your life before!'

'You're right. I haven't. So this should be a learning curve for me. On a number of counts.' He stood up. 'We've got fifteen minutes. Would anyone like anything to eat?'

Melissa was acutely conscious of him during the movie. Lucy had made sure to be the first in the row. Consequently Melissa had found herself stuck in the middle, clutching an enormous bag of salted popcorn into which Elliot's hand dipped at regular intervals, occasionally brushing against hers. Just as well she had seen this particular movie already because she wouldn't have taken much of it in.

She couldn't wait for it to be over. Whenever she tried to rest her arm on the armrest, she felt his and immediately withdrew. When she did manage to relax she would suddenly feel his arm brush hers, the warmth of his skin making her pulses race.

She blamed Alison. She had been fine before. Yes, she had known Elliot was sexy, but in a detached way. Now she kept thinking about that warning, to stay away from him.

It was a blessed relief when the whole experience was at an end and they were outside, back in the waning sunshine with lots of space to manoeuvre.

Lucy was abnormally subdued and it was only when they reached the apartment block that Melissa discovered why. It emerged as a statement but was laden with curiosity.

'I can't believe you've never been to see a Disney movie!'

'In my days there were no cinemas. We kids all had to make do with playing with our tin soldiers and making games for ourselves. No television, you know,' Elliot joked drily.

'Stop lying!'

'OK. I'm not that ancient. I just didn't go to movies as a kid. Nothing strange about that.'

Lucy was reluctant to take the bait, but in the end she couldn't help herself. Curiosity got the better of her. 'Your parents must have taken you to the cinema!'

'My parents lived abroad. They led hectic, cosmopolitan lives. Movies with their kid never featured. Now that I've discovered what I've been missing, I shall have to go out and buy the entire Disney collection.' He was joking and if Melissa wasn't mistaken there was just the dawning of something like a smile on Lucy's face, not that she was going to give in to any sign of warmth. And neither did Elliot expect it. He merely asked them whether they wanted to have a meal with him at the restaurant on the corner and shrugged when his daughter rejected the offer without a second's thought.

'In that case, it'll have to be just the two of us,' he said, turning to Melissa.

'I must get back home,' she said, colour rushing into her face, thinking back to the way her body had felt as though it were on fire every time his arm had unwittingly come into contact with hers during that wretched movie.

'Why?'

'I have things to do!'

'What things?' He took a couple of steps towards her and she wanted to flee.

'Things!'

'When are you going to start Lucy on an exercise programme?'

Melissa's wildly beating heart slowed to a more normal rate. Work. He wanted to go out and have a meal with her so that he could discuss work, most probably to point out that she should be doing what she was being paid to do and not having jolly little outings at his expense. Elliot was a man whose life was ruled by the acquisition of money and power. Naturally he would be concerned that he was in the process of tipping money down the drain.

'It's only been a couple of days...'

'Tell me about it over dinner.' He vanished towards Lucy's bedroom and reappeared minutes later. The jacket was still off but as he walked out into the sitting room he began undoing the buttons of his shirt, starting at the collar and working his way downwards.

Melissa looked at him with alarm. Where the buttons

were now undone, she could glimpse a slither of hard, muscular chest.

'What are you doing?' she stammered, gulping, and Elliot stopped directly in front of her and looked at her with amusement.

'What do you think I'm doing?' He really would have to stop this crazy desire to see her flustered, he thought. He noticed the way her eyes were glued to his face. What did she think they might encounter if they travelled south? He carried on removing his shirt, slowly releasing the cuffs from their cuff-links.

'I'm just going to have a quick shower before we go out,' he said lazily. 'Won't be ten minutes.'

'If you like I can meet you at the restaurant,' Melissa said, eyes still riveted to his face because now the shirt was off and she was just too conscious of the broad, firm expanse of his bronzed chest. He had a superb physique, not too overdeveloped but with fine-honed muscle giving his torso breathtaking definition.

'Don't be silly. In fact, why don't you have a shower yourself? There are two guest bathrooms; you can have your pick.'

Just the thought of stripping off under the same roof as him was enough to give her a mild attack of the vapours. She imagined herself naked under the running water, while on the other side of the sitting room he was the same, naked and...

She gathered herself. 'No, thank you. I'll just go and see what Lucy's up to. She...she's probably hungry, wondering what she might eat a bit later on...what better time to give her a short lecture on nutrition? Not that teenagers are in the least bothered by what they eat...' During the meandering ramble, she had managed to take a couple of steps backwards, which was good and bad. On the one hand, she was no longer breathing the scent of him in, like a drowning man gulping down his last lungfuls of fresh air. On the other hand, she now had a much more all-encompassing view of his semi-nudity, which her eyes insisted on taking in, against all commands from her brain.

He allowed her all the time in the world to finish talking then looked at her in silence for a few seconds. He felt charged. Why?

'Well, if you change your mind, Lucy will point you in the direction of the towels…' He turned away, whistling under his breath, and Melissa remained rooted to the spot until he had disappeared completely, then she collapsed onto the sofa in a heap. Her breathing was rapid and painful, like someone who had just finished a five-mile walk up a steep hill. Had he noticed? she wondered anxiously. More importantly, was this any way for a sensible working woman to behave?

She composed herself enough to go and pay a little visit to Lucy, who she eventually found after a trial-and-error exercise, in the bedroom at the very end of the apartment. Because the apartment ran the entire length of three huge converted Georgian houses, it was sprawling. She stuck her head into several bedrooms, a sitting room and two bathrooms, and finally knocked on the right door to find Lucy sprawled out on her bed with books scattered around her.

'I've decided to go on a diet,' Lucy said, rolling to her side and propping herself up on one elbow. 'Just look at how skinny I used to be.' She nodded to a picture framed on the dressing table of a girl sandwiched between an attractive woman and a fair-haired man wearing wire-rimmed spectacles.

'Your parents?' Melissa asked, picking up the photo and inspecting it.

'Well, one of them.' A long sigh punctuated this remark. 'It's awful to think that I never knew that Brian wasn't my real dad. I keep thinking back, wondering how they could have lied to me all those years.'

'I guess sometimes if you don't tell the truth at the right time, it just gets more and more difficult.'

'Where is he?'

'Having a shower. We're…actually, your father's asked me out to dinner. I think he wants to have a chat about the fact that I haven't got around to chaining you to a treadmill.'

They looked at each other and grinned. 'You were awfully thin,' Melissa said, returning the photo to the dressing table. 'Lucky old you. I used to long for a figure like that when I was your age.'

'Did you?' Lucy seemed pleased by the compliment.

'Short and big-breasted was never much of a fashion statement. There were so many clothes I just couldn't wear. Anyway, I'm glad to hear that you're going on a diet but we'll have to have a chat about that tomorrow. You have to lose weight sensibly or else you'll just end up putting it all back on the minute you start eating properly again.'

'I won't. I just have to cut out all the junk I've spent the last six months piling into my stomach.'

'We'll talk tomorrow, I promise. What are you going to eat tonight?'

'Salad, I suppose. Yuk. I can't stand tomatoes and please don't tell me that they're very good for you. Where is he taking you out to dinner? Somewhere cheap and cheerful, I expect,' she answered her own question in the same breath. 'I can't imagine he would waste much money on the help. Sorry, but it's true. He escorts the witch to all the expensive restaurants, but then again he is trying to impress her.'

Melissa couldn't imagine Elliot trying to impress anyone, but she bit down the remark. Being referred to as *the help* had stung, although it was essentially true. 'They *are* engaged,' she pointed out reasonably. 'Naturally he's going to want to take her out to smart places.'

'You mean she wouldn't dream of putting a foot anywhere that wasn't,' Lucy retorted. 'Just his type.'

'How can you tell what type of woman he likes?' Melissa was drawn into the conversation against her will and only came to her senses when her brain did a rethink of the question. It was no business of hers what type of woman the man went for and it was crazy to try and elicit opinions from his teenage daughter, who had her own enormous axe to grind with him anyway.

'Good question.'

Neither of them had heard Elliot coming. Maybe they had been too involved in their own conversation and so his deep, cool voice had Melissa spinning round to face him. His hair was still slightly damp from the shower and he had changed into a pair of cream trousers, loafers and cream shirt that hung outside the waistband of his trousers. The colours of the clothes did something for him, made him look darker and more exotic.

Lucy shrugged and returned to her mound of school books, which she flicked through with sudden, frowning concentration, little realising that that in itself was the clearest signal she could have given that she was paying absolutely no attention to what was in front of her. Elliot passed his usual courteous remarks, which met with the usual grunt of non-acknowledgement, and then he stood back to let Melissa walk past him.

The brief thaw Melissa had noticed in Lucy after the cinema had vanished and the frost was back in full force. She tried to imagine three more months of atmosphere, but instead of feeling dismayed she felt a certain level of excitement. Her curiosity had been piqued, she decided, had lured her into the situation almost when her back was turned.

And, dislikeable though she found Elliot, really, he was the most stimulating man she had ever come into contact with. Maybe it was to do with the hum of energy that vibrated around him. Her eyes slid over him, taking in his arresting sexiness, and she felt a guilty stirring in her veins.

In an attempt to cover it up, she launched into an animated spiel about his apartment, asking a series of banal questions about the décor, how long he had lived there, whether he enjoyed living in London, didn't sometimes long to get away from the fast pace of city life.

Throughout this she managed to avoid direct eye contact, preferring to gaze ahead of her in the lift and breathing a little sigh of relief when they finally stepped outside into the evening air, which was still clinging to some remnants of warmth.

'And I guess you want to ask me about my plans for Lucy,' she continued, effortlessly filling any potential for a gap in the conversation.

'In due course,' Elliot murmured. He signalled for a taxi.

'Where are we going? I thought we were just going to pop into the Italian on the corner. The cheap and cheerful place,' she reminded him, with a question in her voice.

'There *are* other cheap and cheerful places around,' he said, opening the door of the cab to let her in and finishing his sentence when he was sitting inside, next to her. 'A French cheap and cheerful might make a change.'

'Are French restaurants ever cheap and cheerful?' There was an enforced intimacy in sitting in the back of the taxi with him that was disturbing. 'I'm not dressed for anything fancy,' she carried on, stammering.

'Won't…well, won't your fiancée mind you taking another woman out for a meal?'

He greeted this question with a slow, amused smile, and Melissa groaned inwardly to herself. Why did she behave like this whenever she was in his company? She was always the picture of cheerful, detached propriety with all the other male members of the gym, even the ones who occasionally made suggestive remarks to her.

'I mean,' Melissa qualified hurriedly, 'this is purely a business date but, you know, some women can be very jealous and I wouldn't want to…be responsible for any unpleasant situation arising between the two of you…' Her voice trailed off and she thought back to the warning Alison had given her the evening before.

'Alison isn't prone to fits of jealousy,' Elliot pointed out.

'You say that but…'

'But what…?' he asked softly, his voice wrapping around her in the hushed bubble of the cab.

'But women can be jealous…' she said feebly.

'That's not what you meant to say. I've noticed you do that when you're feeling nervous.'

'Do what?'

'This.' He reached forward and tucked some wildly straying blonde hair behind her ear. For a few seconds, shock at the unexpected gesture made her go completely still.

A crazy thought leapt into Elliot's head. How would she react if he did somewhat more than just flick a few strands of hair away from her face? How would she be if he touched her? Really touched her?

He laughed at himself a little incredulously.

'So? Going to tell me what you meant to say?' he continued teasingly.

'I think you might find that your fiancée is a little more

jealous than you think,' Melissa stuttered. She kept her hands firmly clutched on her lap to resist the urge to give in to the nervous gesture he had just commented upon.

'And you get that idea from…where?'

Melissa felt like a rabbit pinned in the headlights of a rapidly approaching car. The fact that the taxi was slowing down, stopping, in front of a chic little restaurant with tables and chairs set outside under umbrellas, was short relief, because as soon as they were shown to their seats he resumed the conversation.

'You were about to tell me why you've come to the conclusion that Alison is jealous or possessive.'

'I really don't like repeating conversations,' she squeaked in a last-ditch attempt to change the subject. He was having none of it. His blue eyes were hard and waiting.

'And I really don't like aspersions being cast on someone's character which are not backed up by some kind of evidence.'

'I wasn't casting any aspersions. I don't see anything wrong with two people who love each other being a little jealous and a little possessive!'

'You're stalling.' He ordered a bottle of wine, keeping one eye on her. 'Do I make you nervous? Stupid question. Of course I do. You act like a cat on a hot tin roof whenever I'm around, but I know that you're not normally like that. When you were recommended to me, the first thing Samantha said was how mature you were for your age, how you hardly ever became rattled by any of the clients, and some of them can be quite…forthcoming, I gather. So, tell me, what is it about me? Does it make you uncomfortable to work for me?'

Melissa nodded vigorously and waited for her vocal cords to return to working order.

'And with regards to your fiancée,' Melissa didn't

want to get involved in any conversations about why Elliot made her nervous, so she opted for the truth about Alison instead '…she told me that I should be encouraging Lucy to consider boarding-school, that it was the best solution given the circumstances, and she also told me that I should make sure…'

'Yes…?' He inclined towards her, absentmindedly taking a sip of the wine being held out for him to taste by the waiter and nodding impatiently when asked whether it could be poured.

'Make sure that I don't get any ideas,' Melissa finished in a rush. 'That some women might find you attractive and that it would be easy for me to become one of them.'

Elliot raised his glass to his lips and sipped, regarding her over the rim with those penetrating blue eyes of his.

'And would it be?' he asked with interest.

Melissa downed a large mouthful of wine. Here she was, floundering again. Was this more urbane conversation? He wasn't really interested, not at all. He only wanted to know what she had to say about her plans for Lucy, because his money was tied up there, but he certainly wasn't concerned by the thought that she might end up being attracted to him. And why on earth should he be? He just wasn't ready to get around to talking about his daughter just yet, and this line of conversation probably appealed to his male ego.

She decided to stamp on any such far-fetched notion. 'No,' she said, shaking her head and smiling. 'Not at all. I've always been able to draw a line between work and play and, anyway, you're not my type at all.' The wine was going down a treat. She suddenly felt very expansive and very self-confident.

'You have a type?' Elliot was enjoying this. He really hadn't noticed exactly how rigid his life was until now. Despite her job, which must have entailed some structure, she seemed by nature a highly unstructured individual and it was certainly a novel and amusing experience to see how she operated. In fact, it was doing his jaded soul a world of good.

'There's a fantastic choice of food,' she murmured, rereading the menu from the top down and realising that her glass had been refilled when she went to have just a tiny sip more.

Elliot grunted. He was intrigued to hear what this type of man was that she was attracted to. Discussing the choice of food on the menu was a tedious interruption. Her hair was doing it again, flopping over her cheek. She had tied it back into a pony-tail but now, without thinking or looking in his direction, she released it and he drew in his breath sharply as the mane of blonde curls scattered down around her shoulders. Suddenly she didn't seem quite so much like the amusing girl-next-door variety.

'Don't you think?' Melissa looked up at him, her wide blue eyes thrilled. 'I suppose you come to places like this all the time, but I don't. In fact, I haven't been to a single smart restaurant since I came down to London.'

Her hair must be a thousand shades of blonde, he thought, trying to pay attention to what she was saying. Some bits were incredibly fair, others were warmer, more like honey.

'Awful, isn't it?'

'I beg your pardon?'

'My hair. I could see you looking at it.' And no doubt comparing it to Alison's sleek black bob, she thought glumly. No points for guessing who had won the Hair Contest. 'Have you decided what you're going to have?'

'Oh. Oh, yes. And incidentally, your hair isn't awful. Far from it. And you were telling me about your type…'

'Well, I thought we'd finished that bit of conversation and moved on to something else. The food. And really, we ought to talk about Lucy. I feel very guilty that I haven't started anything dramatic as yet. I know that you're paying me and I promise you that I'll do a good job…'

'I'm sure you will. She seems to have taken to you already.' Reluctantly, Elliot dragged his mind back into focus. Luckily there was no need for him to concentrate too hard because after the best part of a bottle of wine, Melissa was doing most of the talking. He could eat his food and allow his eyes to drift lazily over her as she indulged in her lamb noisettes with a gusto he had never before seen in a woman, while she happily chatted about her lack of experience in fine dining, described her plans for Lucy, told him all about her past working as a nanny and laughing at various episodes that had taken place, and making him laugh as well.

'You're staring at me,' Melissa finally said as her plate was taken away, scraped clean. 'I suppose finishing every last morsel of food on your plate isn't really the done thing in an expensive restaurant, is it?' She looked momentarily sheepish at the thought. 'It was absolutely delicious, though. I don't get to do much cooking where I am. I've not much of a kitchen, actually.'

'I think it's very…rare but engaging to see a woman actually finish eating everything on her plate.'

Melissa suddenly didn't feel rare or engaging. She felt awkward and lumpish. 'And their figures show it,' she laughed, realising that she was now hardly a walking advert for moderation in one's eating habits, which would be what she would have to instil in Lucy presumably. At least she had resisted the dessert menu and had drunk her coffee decaffeinated and black. She thought of the long, slender Alison and felt a nasty twinge of jealousy.

'Do you have a problem with your figure?'

'Don't all women?' Melissa sidestepped the question.

The room was beginning to spin ever so slightly and when she stood up at the end of the meal she found she had to grip the back of her chair to steady herself.

Elliot was on his feet before she could sit back down, holding her by the waist. 'Sudden onset of flu, do you think,' he murmured softly into her ear, 'or a little too much wine?'

His breath was warm and gave her the most wonderful, squirmy sensation in her stomach.

'Ha, ha. I don't normally drink. I'm fine now. You can let me go. I promise I won't embarrass you by falling in a heap on the floor.'

'Very little embarrasses me and that certainly wouldn't.' His arms remained exactly where they were, supporting her, and together they walked towards the door, only stopping so that he could pay the bill. Even when he was writing out the slip, one arm stayed around her, his hand only inches away from the curve of her breast, and Melissa was horrified to realise that her body was responding to him, nipples tautening against her sensible cotton bra.

'Where are you taking me?' she asked drowsily. Her eyelids felt like two pieces of lead, and with a little sigh she slumped against him in the back of the taxi, which he must have summoned without her noticing. His deep, lazy drawl seemed to reach her from miles away.

'Where would you like to be taken?'

She felt his fingers curl into her hair and she closed her eyes and yawned. She wondered vaguely how a little bit of wine could have mellowed her so much that she felt absolutely wonderful lying against Elliot and feeling his hands in her hair.

'I'm taking you home,' he said softly, 'your home.'

'You don't know where I live.'

'I know everything.' He laughed under his breath. 'Including where you live.'

Melissa could feel her eyes getting heavier and heavier and the next time she opened them she was looking at the walls of the stairwell in her house travelling past her, even though she didn't appear to be moving. She realised that she was being carried up the stairs and she made a token effort to dislodge herself.

'Ah. You're up,' Elliot commented lightly.

'You'll damage your back carrying me.'

'I could take that as a slur on my virility,' Elliot murmured huskily.

Except, of course, he never would, she thought. Because he was as virile as they came. She could feel the muscles of his arms lifting her and the corded strength of his neck under her hands. Lord only knew when he had managed to get her keys from her—probably when they were in the taxi and he was thinking clearly while she slumbered in total abandonment against him.

He fiddled with the lock on her door without putting her down before kicking it open and then stepping inside.

'God,' he muttered incredulously, 'you live *here*?'

Melissa yawned and giggled. 'Wonderful, isn't it? I call it cosy and compact.'

'Where's your bed?'

'The thing with the cushions on it.'

He laid her down and then stood up and looked around him in disgust while Melissa watched his reactions through half-closed eyes. She felt crazily alive and suddenly very daring. The wine had gone to her head but had not tipped her over the edge, and although her head was still swimming a bit, her senses were on full alert.

'I'll leave you now,' he said, when his inspection of her tiny room was over. 'You need to get out of your clothes and get some sleep.'

The sidelight he had switched on was buzzing with its usual inefficiency. That was something that had always bugged her because she needed to switch on both table lamps whenever she wanted to actually see what she was doing, but right now the subdued lighting suited her just fine.

'Would you make me some coffee?' she heard herself ask, and after a moment's hesitation he nodded and disappeared into the kitchenette, where she could hear the clink of a mug being fetched from the cupboard and the hissing of the kettle as it gathered steam.

Her clothes felt tight and uncomfortable now that she was lying down.

On sudden, urgent impulse she began wriggling out of them, eager to get some cool air on her body. Every bit of her was on fire and a languorous feeling of utter wantonness swept through her as she heard him switch off the kitchen light.

CHAPTER SIX

MELISSA saw Elliot stop in shock. For a few seconds he looked as though his brain had received information which it was finding difficult to decipher, then it all clicked together and he approached her slowly.

One small part of her was desperately trying to reassert some reason, but it was fighting a losing battle against the greater part that was wildly turned on and fuelled by a desire she had never felt in her life before. That wicked part of her now made her stretch out, extending her body on the sofa bed and watching him as he finally came to stand in front of her, over her, the mug of coffee incongruously in his hand.

'What the hell are you doing?' he rasped.

'You said I needed to get undressed.' His voice was harsh but his eyes roamed over her and his scrutiny made her blood heat.

'You've had way too much to drink. It was my fault. I should have stopped you.'

'Why? You might be my employer but I'm a big girl and you're not my moral guardian.' She was speaking slowly, making sure that she didn't trip over her words.

With an indecipherable oath, Elliot dumped the coffee on the mantelpiece and began gathering her clothes from the floor. He seemed to have second thoughts and asked her roughly to point him in the direction of her pyjamas.

His normally superb cool was shattered. He was making a good attempt to gather it but she could tell from his jerky movements that he wasn't succeeding. It gave her a feeling of heady power.

When she failed to supply him with the information he had requested, he went to the chest of drawers, pulling each one open until he had located the one that contained the oversized T-shirts that she used as nightwear. He yanked out the first one that came to hand and seemed to inhale deeply before he turned round.

Elliot knew what he should do. He should just drop the T-shirt on top of her and bid her goodnight. She had been capable of removing her clothes so she shouldn't have any problem putting some on.

But when he looked…

He felt a rush of attraction that was so powerful it nearly rocked him on his feet. Her tangled blonde hair seemed unnaturally light against the dark cushion and her body was smooth as satin.

He perched on the side of the sofa bed. 'Come on. Sit up and I'll stick this on you, or else…'

'Or else what?' Melissa obediently sat up but she didn't take the T-shirt from him. Instead she propped herself up on her hands so that her breasts were thrust out at him, ripe, delectable fruit waiting to be picked.

Elliot groaned under his breath and went to put the shirt over her, his hand grazing her breasts as he did so.

The contact of his hand against her nipples was electrifying. Melissa let her head drop back and closed her eyes. She heard him mutter something forcefully under his breath, then she felt his mouth against hers, pushing her back, claiming her with white-hot, driving urgency.

He dropped the T-shirt. With frantic hands, Melissa began undoing the buttons of his shirt so that she could slide her hands against his chest and feel the hardness of his torso.

'Oh, God,' he muttered thickly, 'this is lunacy.' But already his hands had found her breast and he was cupping it, massaging it roughly, rubbing the tip of his thumb over her sensitised nipple.

'Yes, oh, yes!' Her own voice sounded oddly strangled. She pushed him down, arching up and releasing a long, shuddering sigh of satisfaction as his mouth covered her throbbing nipple, drawing it in, licking and sucking and teasing. Her body couldn't keep still. She moved sensuously against him and the roughness of his trousers sent shivers of excitement racing through her heated body.

When he had finished with one breast, he began his exquisite plundering of the other and then his hand was on her inner thigh, stroking its smoothness, edging higher. With a gasp, Melissa parted her legs, waiting for those clever, experienced fingers to touch her, in the grip of the most overwhelming roller-coaster ride of sensation she had ever experienced.

She moaned when he finally did touch her there, in her most intimate place, rhythmically rubbing while she writhed against his fingers, offering her breasts to his warm mouth and everything else to his expert exploration.

Like a flower that suddenly began to bloom, she was besieged by a feeling of newness, of her body opening up and becoming alive for the first time ever. She reached for him, seeking out the hardness she felt pressed like a rod of iron against her, but it was too late. The swollen bud he was rubbing was already soaring towards fulfilment and with a cry she reached the pinnacle of enjoyment, which seemed to last forever. She stiffened and pressed her hand to the back of his head, urging his mouth against her breast as wave after wave of pleasure rocked her.

All trace of wine had disappeared from her veins when she next opened her eyes to meet his staring down at her.

'I think it's time I left, don't you?' Elliot's voice was unsteady and he was already standing up, drawing away from her.

Suddenly the room felt icy cold to Melissa. Reality was piecing itself together slowly but surely and it wasn't pleasant. In fact, it was a nightmare. She hooked the throw around her and watched with growing mortification as he buttoned up his shirt, making sure not to glance at her at all.

What had happened to the wild, soaring recklessness that had consumed her? Where had it gone? Its rapid departure had left her with a picture she could scarcely bear to look at. An image of a foolish woman throwing herself at a man who was unavailable, a man for whom she worked, someone who had not once shown the slightest glimmer of attraction towards her. Her mind screeched to a halt before she could contemplate the awfulness of it in too much detail.

She struggled up to sit and curled herself protectively under the throw, pulling up her legs and propping her face on her knees.

'I'm sorry.' She made herself talk as loudly as possible. She also forced herself to look directly at him because this wasn't some casual one-night stand she could leave behind forever with a sigh of relief. This was someone she would be seeing again and again over the next few months.

'Save it,' Elliot said harshly. 'I should be the one apologising. You had too much to drink and I took advantage of you.'

Melissa didn't say anything. She tucked her hair behind her ears and then stopped when she remembered what he had said about noticing how she did that every time she was nervous. It seemed like a lifetime ago since he had uttered that statement. Her eyes left his and she stared miserably down at the ground, waiting while the silence gathered around her like treacle.

Eventually she heard the quiet click of the door being closed and when she looked up it was to find that Elliot had gone, leaving her alone to painfully consider the implications of what she had done.

And also her options.

They were simple. She could either stay and spend the next few weeks in a state of painful suspension with his presence reminding her daily of her own stupidity. Or she could go. She had never set eyes on him in the gym before and it was entirely likely that she never would again, especially now that she knew exactly when he tended to go there. That way there would be no uncomfortable confrontations and no chance for her own attraction to him to grow, not if he wasn't around. And Lucy…well, Lucy would probably be relieved in a way that she was again free to do what she wanted without being overseen by someone her father had seen fit to put in place.

Alison had warned her against falling for his considerable sex appeal. At the time she had laughed off the warning. It was to her shame that she had gone and done just the thing she had dismissed as ridiculous.

Sleep eventually claimed her before her thoughts could fully switch off and she slept fitfully, waking at the crack of dawn and experiencing a few seconds of blissful amnesia before the sickening memories of the night before descended with remorseless speed.

Some time in the night she had arrived at her decision, and before getting dressed she sat down and composed her bland letter of resignation.

Then she went to work at the health club, as usual.

If anyone noticed a change in her, no one commented, and by the end of the day she assumed that whatever was going through her head, it certainly wasn't showing on her face or in her demeanour.

She had no idea when he would be at the apartment, and as soon as her last client for the day had gone, instead of catching up on some paperwork, she went across to the manager's office, to which she was allowed free access as a member of staff. Fortunately Samantha wasn't there to ask any piercing questions, and her secretary was accustomed to Melissa coming in, having a look at files and updating them with information.

She didn't pay a scrap of notice when Melissa fished out Elliot's file and noted down his office address. Nor did she bat an eyelid when she told her that she would be leaving early to catch up with some paperwork.

Elliot's office was in the City. It only occurred to Melissa belatedly, when she was standing outside the imposing building, that there was a better than average chance that he wouldn't be in. Or if he was in, he would be in one of those high-powered meetings he seemed to enjoy so much.

I'll just have to wait, she decided. It wouldn't be nice, not when she was prepared with her letter in her bag, but she couldn't possibly wait for him at the apartment if it was one of his late nights. Lucy would be curious and then there was the strong possibility that she would overhear part of their conversation, which would be a disaster.

She took a deep breath and walked through the large revolving glass door, to find herself confronted with acres of marble. At this hour it was relatively quiet, but as offices went there was, she realised, next to no chance that she would be allowed up to his office to wait for him. And this was confirmed when the woman at the reception desk, having looked her up and down, informed her that no one was allowed in without an appointment.

The letter of resignation was burning a hole in her bag.

'I'm afraid I won't be leaving until I see Mr Jay,' Melissa said stubbornly.

'Mr Jay is an extremely busy man.' Her name badge proclaimed her to be Ms Cribbs and she certainly looked like a Ms Very Icy and was very determined not to allow any ordinary mortals access to one of her important directors.

'I'm sure he is,' Melissa said tartly, 'but...' she lowered her voice and allowed a few seconds of meaningful silence to stretch between them '...I think you'll find that he'll be very angry *indeed* if he learns that you've asked me to leave. *Very angry indeed.*'

Their eyes met and the woman hesitated for a second or two. 'I take it your visit is of a personal nature?' she enquired coldly.

'Of an *extremely personal nature*,' Melissa said, enunciating each word with deliberate slowness.

'Hold on a minute.' She didn't want to do it, but the thought of incurring Elliot's wrath was obviously too much. She picked up the phone, spoke for a few minutes in hushed tones, back half-turned to Melissa, and then replaced the receiver. 'Mr Jay is in a meeting but his secretary has given permission for you to wait for him in his offices. He's on the fourth floor. She'll be waiting for you by the lift. You do understand,' she continued stiffly, 'that in an organisation such as this, stray members of the public are not allowed to wander through the building unchecked.'

Tense though she was, Melissa nearly grinned at the thought that her unprepossessing attire might well have engendered the *stray members of the public* remark. Amongst these high-level business people in their dark suits and crisp white shirts, her light blue summer skirt and sandals stuck out like a sore thumb.

'I quite understand,' Melissa said solemnly. 'Fourth floor?'

'Mrs Watkins will be there.'

There was the general smell of money being made in these offices. There were two people in the lift Melissa took up. Neither spoke and nor did they look at each other. The woman was dressed in a sober grey suit, with high heels and the regulation white blouse, and the man was in a pinstripe suit. They stared ahead of them, both sporting identical little frowns, while Melissa stood between and slightly behind, a great vantage point from which to observe how the other half operated.

There was no time for Melissa to feel really nervous until the lift doors opened on to the fourth floor and there was the fabled Mrs Watkins, waiting for her. She, too, was in a suit but, because she was in her fifties, her clothing was not quite so imposing. She also had a friendly face that displayed no hint of curiosity. Though curious she must certainly be, Melissa thought. After all, who could this woman in the summer skirt be, there to see the great Elliot Jay on *a personal matter that couldn't wait*?

'I haven't been able to interrupt Mr Jay at his meeting,' she confided, ushering Melissa into an office within an office. 'But it's scheduled to finish in about half an hour. Perhaps you might like a cup of tea or coffee while you wait?'

'I'll just wait,' Melissa said, and contemplate my behaviour last night for the millionth time, she added silently to herself.

'I'll be out there if you need me.'

Once the other woman had gone, Melissa looked around her with interest. She was seeing another side to Elliot. This was the side that really showed how powerful he was. The carpeting was lush and his offices seemed to have been designed with a process of filtration in mind.

Outer office number one appeared to house a few crucial secretaries, who had barely glanced up when she and Mrs Watkins had passed through. Just off this outer office was Mrs Watkins' own, small, private office, complete with walnut desk, computer, phones and a flowering pot plant. Through the outer office was the room in which Melissa now sat. This was clearly a waiting area for clients, and a very tasteful one at that. Of course, she thought, it wouldn't do to allow any hint of his personality to intrude. The pictures on the walls were bland sketches of London, the two small sofas were beige, to match the carpet, and the squat coffee-table was of smooth, blonde wood that bore not a single stain or mark. People sat here to discuss matters of importance. The last thing they needed would be any visual distractions.

And beyond this room, she assumed, was Elliot's own office, to which the door was shut. Through two long glass panels she could make out an enormous desk, the obligatory computer, phones, a fax machine and files. In her head, she perked it up with some plants, a dashing *faux* leopard-skin rug and a comfortable reclining chair, in matching leopard skin. It was an amusing game and it managed to take her mind off things just long enough for her to miss his arrival. One minute she was squinting through the glass panels and mentally redecorating his office, the next she had turned around and there he was, framed in the doorway, staring at her.

How did he manage to do that? He was dressed in the same sober charcoal grey suit as everyone else, but he didn't look like a drone. He looked all man. Dark, powerful and unsmiling.

Having prepared herself for this meeting and rehearsed in her head all the cool things she would say, Melissa now felt sick with tension and overwhelmed with disgraceful memories. She could still feel his hands on her, touching her at her own invitation, sending her senses flying in every direction while he played with the most intimate part of her body. She licked her lips, half stood up and then sat back down on the sofa.

'What are you doing here, Melissa?' He strode into the room and shut the door behind him. Instead of sitting down, though, he simply stood behind one of the sofas and leaned forward, propping himself up on his hands.

'I've come to deliver this to you.' Melissa rummaged in her bag, found the envelope and held it out shakily.

'What is it?'

'Read it.'

Elliot pushed himself up, opened the envelope and sat on the sofa facing her, reading her carefully worded letter of resignation slowly, then he placed it on the table between them and looked at her.

'Why do you feel that under the circumstances your position is untenable?'

'I haven't come here to take up your valuable time with long explanations,' Melissa told him quietly.

'Oh, I think I can decide how I want to use my valuable time, and right now I'm very interested in hearing your explanation. What happened last night was a mistake, I'll grant you that, but mistakes happen and there's no reason for this particular one to affect your contract of employment.'

'And I don't think that an apology is good enough.' She could feel her cheeks burning and she looked away, past him to the door he had shut. She just couldn't bring herself to meet those shuttered blue eyes. 'I behaved abominably.'

'You drank a little too much; it went to your head. These things happen. I should have had more control, while we're pointing fingers, and I think we both realise that.' He was grimly aware that he had never felt so out of control in his life before. In a life where parameters were firmly drawn and nothing ever got out of hand or found him floundering, his experience the night before had left a disturbing, sour taste in his mouth. He hadn't for a single second thought about Alison. In retrospect, that said it all about their relationship, gave him the message loud and clear that, however convenient their arrangement was and however much he liked her, marriage to Alison was out of the question. He would break it to her later. Right now, he had his own anger with himself to deal with.

'It still makes things very awkward for me,' Melissa said. 'I really don't see how we can continue having any sort of professional relationship.'

'Why? Because you think you might be tempted to fling yourself at me again?'

Melissa's mouth dropped open at the sheer nerve of the remark. Who the hell did he think he was? Universal sex god? Did he imagine that she had been secretly lusting after him and then she had thrown herself at him because she just couldn't resist any longer?

'Your silence is illuminating.'

Melissa snapped shut her mouth and glared at him. 'I'm just staggered that you could think that. I know that wine isn't much of an excuse but I can't hold my drink very well.'

'In other words, I could have been anyone?'

No, her mind screamed. 'Who knows?' she said, shrugging.

'In which case I suggest you make sure that you drink alcohol well away from the public at large or you might find yourself in a situation you hadn't quite bargained on.' Elliot's mouth tightened. He wasn't vain. He certainly didn't spend hours preening himself in front of a mirror, nor did he carry a comb in his back pocket for emergency situations when he might just need to spruce himself up. However, he did know that women singled him out. The implication that he was merely in the right place at the right time stuck in his throat.

'Let's be logical about this,' Elliot said grimly, leaning forward to rest his elbows on his knees. 'From what I see, you're doing a good job with Lucy. You're far more of a companion to her than Lenka has ever been, and you may well be the stepping stone to help her through this period. And, judging by the state of your bedsit, you clearly need the money, if only to save up so that you can afford something slightly more salubrious in due course.'

'That's not the point…'

'No, it's not the point, but these are things that are strongly in favour of you staying on for the duration. You say that you don't feel that you can maintain a normal working relationship with me after what happened…' He could see mortification stamped on her face like a brand, and he knew that it was a measure of her inexperience. To have derived pleasure from the circumstances in which she had found herself was a bitter pill she had to swallow and he could have kicked himself be-cause…because…

Because she deserved to have pleasure in the right cir-cumstances. With the right man, he told himself.

'I don't see the point of talking about it,' Melissa whis-pered, staring at the table now.

'Of course we have to talk about it,' Elliot snapped impatiently. 'There's no sense in beating yourself up for a crime you haven't committed. As we've already estab-lished, it was a mistake. I'm not your type of man any more than you are my type of woman.' Something nig-gled at the back of his mind and he ignored it. 'But some-times things happen. I promise you that when you leave this room, you leave this conversation, and what happened between us, behind. No more will be mentioned on the subject. You could say that it never happened.'

I could never say that, Melissa thought in dismay. Because it *did* happen and it will keep on happening in my head. What was wrong with her? Why couldn't she just laugh about it and then consign the episode to history?

'It's not the end of the world, Melissa,' Elliot interrupted her thoughts, his voice husky and incisive. 'Haven't you ever done anything that was…shall we say, regrettable?'

'What do you mean?'

'I mean, have you never indulged in a wild sexual experience just for the hell of it?'

'No!' Melissa was shocked. 'I'm sorry but I simply don't see the point of that and, anyway, casual sex is not good for one's health.'

'You don't think it has some benefits?' Elliot's mouth curved into a slow, sexy smile that sent shivers racing up and down her spine.

'Maybe for someone else but not for me.' She stood up and cleared her throat. 'OK. I'll stay on working for you because, as you point out, I think Lucy and I are beginning to forge a bond, which is good, and because I need the money. Or rather, the extra money would be very helpful, but you have to give me your word that none of this…what happened…is ever mentioned again.'

'I already have given you my word.'

For the time being at any rate, Elliot thought, watching her as she hovered there, anxiously wondering whether she had done the right thing. In due course, the subject of sex would be raised again because she roused his curiosity.

'You'll be gone by the time I get back tonight,' he

said, standing up and ushering her to the door. 'What are you planning to do with Lucy?' His mind was already zooming ahead to what he himself had to do later as Melissa spent a few minutes outlining her plans. She knew he was barely listening to a word she was saying. His expression was frowning, distracted.

Was he thinking about whatever meeting he had planned for later? Maybe he was going to be seeing Alison. That thought arrested her flow of conversation. 'I don't know how to say this…' she began and after a few seconds the sound of her prolonged silence finally regained his attention. He focused on her once again, although the frown was still there.

'Say what?'

'And I know we both made a pact never to drag this subject up again, but…'

Elliot tore his mind away from the uncomfortable evening that lay ahead. He hoped that Alison wouldn't kick up a fuss when he broke the news that it was all over between them. The fact that he would be unable to give any concrete reason why their relationship was at an end would not be helpful. Women liked reasons. Still, he didn't imagine that she would shed any tears. She was a high-powered barrister, insured against emotionalism. Sobbing would not be her scene. But the recriminations would be bad enough.

'Drag…drag what?' Elliot murmured, barely registering what she had said.

'When you see your fiancée, I would appreciate it if you didn't mention what happened between us… I know I'm encouraging you to be deceitful, but I really would appreciate it, at least while I'm working under your roof…'

'Fair enough,' Elliot said, thinking that really that little episode would be irrelevant anyway, considering his fiancée would be no more as of tonight. He watched as her shoulders sagged in relief.

Melissa was a study in ingenuity. Every emotion was written on her face. She had missed the toughening-up pill that most girls swallowed when they were teenagers, the one that made them adept at concealment, that turned them into women who could handle the occasional lapse and laugh it off in an adult, carefree manner, that turned them into the sort of women that he had always dated.

He looked at her speculatively. He had a meeting in ten minutes' time but suddenly his purely masculine curiosity got the better of him. He poked his head out of the office door and told his secretary that he would be running slightly late for his meeting.

'Oh, no,' Melissa said anxiously, 'I've already used up enough of your time. You have…important things to do…'

Elliot closed the door and signalled for her to sit back down. 'Nothing that won't wait for me.'

'Because you're…'

'So very, very important.' He gave her a crooked smile, coaxing a tentative one in return, and then moved to sit next to her on the sofa. He couldn't really work out what it was about this woman, but she intrigued him. In the space of only a few days, for a start, she had made him aware of shortcomings in his relationship with Alison that he had not consciously been aware of. Then again, thinking about it, how often did he and Alison meet, spend time together? Juggling evenings with their joint busy schedules was a tricky procedure, prone to cancellations, something which he had happily lived with and indeed accepted as perfectly normal. They had good sex, when they got around to it, but was it magnificent?

'Believe me, I understand your doubts about us continuing to work together.'

'Do you?' Melissa eyed him sceptically. This was not the kind of conversation she wanted to be having. She certainly didn't want him sitting so close to her. He was facing her and she was acutely, alarmingly aware of his proximity. Everything was so vibrantly, intensely *male* about him that simply breathing in the scent of him made her feel a bit faint. She made a few edgy movements and came up against the solid barrier of the sofa arm.

'I do.' He placed one hand soothingly over hers and Melissa felt as though she had suddenly received a massive electric charge. This is exactly what I'm talking about! she wanted to shriek. Last night was hideous enough, but worse still was that it had brought with it, along with all the expected feelings of mortification and abject embarrassment, an overriding awareness of him as a man, which was something she had done her level best to ignore since she had first set eyes on him. She awkwardly tried to slide her hand out from under his. To no avail.

'It's very important that you don't harbour any wariness where I am concerned. You have to be free to have an unconditional relationship with me, safe in the knowledge that you can tell me anything.' Elliot continued to rest his hand on hers.

Unconditional? Melissa considered that a poor choice of word.

'OK.'

Elliot frowned. 'So we understand each other?'

'I think so.' Actually, the only thing she was currently thinking was how much she wanted to escape the suffocating impact of his presence. She thought about telling him that she had changed her mind, had decided that she couldn't possibly work for him after all, but that would have been pathetic. She had painted herself into a corner

and now she would just have to sit through his kindly
lecture as best she could.

'There can be no room for you avoiding me.'

'I wouldn't do that,' Melissa lied, blushing. 'How
could I? I would have to deliver Lucy back to your apartment and I wouldn't duck behind the kitchen counter if
I heard your key in the door.' But she would have to
fight the temptation, she acceded to herself. With the way
her body behaved when she was around him, the option
of unglamorously squatting behind a counter to hide
would be almost irresistible. She thanked her lucky stars
that Elliot wasn't a mind-reader as well as everything
else. If he had been, he would have spotted in seconds
how powerfully he affected her.

That was something which he could never be allowed
to see. To have him aware of the fact would scupper any
chance of that perfectly normal, unconditional, feel-free-
to-talk-to-me boss-employee relationship he was recom-
mending.

'I'm relieved to hear it,' Elliot said drily, meeting her
eyes and holding her gaze. He removed his hand and
noted how hers speedily went to her lap, well out of
harm's way. 'I admit that I won't be making a habit of
coming home at six, but I will want weekly reports of
how you're doing with Lucy. A run-down of what you've
been up to.'

With the conversation back on a work footing, Melissa
allowed herself to relax. She nodded, eager to be gone.
For someone whose working life was so meticulously
ordered, Elliot's line of conversation always seemed to
contain an unsettling air of unpredictability. Was that part
of his compelling fascination?

'Of course,' Melissa agreed promptly.

'I think Fridays would be good for that, don't you
agree?'

'Yes, that would be fine.'

'I know it can be an awkward day. Most young women want to celebrate the end of the week by going out partying...' He dropped his eyes and sat back, leaving this tantalising carrot dangling in the air between them.

'If I know what time you'll want me to stay until, then I'll make sure that I'm available. But can you arrange your working hours to suit? I thought you found it difficult to take time off...'

'Up till now, I admit I haven't been around for Lucy,' Elliot said heavily. 'I've done all the things that needed to be done, made sure that she got into a good school, arranged for a personal shopper to kit her out in whatever clothes she wanted, bought her whatever she needed or asked for, but I failed to put in any time with her.' Alison hadn't helped. Had she felt threatened by the sudden appearance of his teenage daughter? He hadn't thought so at the time, but in retrospect it made sense. She had maintained a firm hand, never once questioning his lack of personal input, and, unaccustomed to having his actions curtailed in any way, Elliot had obligingly gone along for the ride.

Melissa thought that if he had come to that point of knowledge, then there might be a chance that they could alter the battle lines that were slowly but surely setting like concrete between Lucy and Elliot before it was too late. She smiled in appreciation of the prospect.

'I'll make sure that I'm back at the apartment by six every Friday,' Elliot continued. It was a suggestion that had come off the top of his head, but now it seemed like a really good idea. 'We can go out for a meal together, the three of us, and then you can spend a few minutes filling me in on what's been happening afterwards.'

'A meal?' Melissa frowned, not too sure how a quick

debriefing once a week had turned into dinner out and her whole evening spoken for.

'Unless you generally have plans for a Friday…? You never said…'

'I…' Suddenly it felt a little abnormal having to admit to Fridays spent in, doing nothing. She had not been in London long enough to make any solid friends, and those she did see she generally saw on a Saturday. 'I…I do sometimes go out on a Friday. Clubbing,' she added, for good measure. 'You know. But I could make sure that I'm available for the next couple of months.'

'*Clubbing?*'

Melissa mumbled something under her breath.

'You go *clubbing*?'

'It's what young people tend to do,' she said defensively. That much was true enough at any rate. Young people did do that. She just didn't happen to be one of them.

'As opposed to dinosaurs like myself?' Elliot grinned slowly and mesmerisingly. That warranted another mumble.

'I'm sure you go to *different* clubs,' Melissa stammered.

'Maybe. We'll have to compare notes one day.' Melissa's face was saying no, but her chest was heaving. He'd love to touch her again—the thought sprang from nowhere and was lost before he could hold it—to touch her slowly, bit by leisurely bit…to send her soaring, but next time without embarrassment and with the right man, yes…him.

CHAPTER SEVEN

ELLIOT stared at his computer screen and impatiently tapped his pen on the black leather pad on which his keyboard rested. He was not accustomed to this, to being at the mercy of feelings he could not identify. It was like an itch that needed scratching. And he had felt like this for the past six weeks.

In his highly focused life, Elliot had always been able to conduct his private life without it overlapping work. He enjoyed women but they never intruded into the intensely enjoyable and demanding area of deals and mergers and the tremendously invigorating and time-consuming business of making a fortune. In fact, it wasn't even about making a fortune. With several already at his disposal, Elliot had become used to working simply for the challenge of it. Women had always filled necessary slots but they just never crossed the threshold. He had always had the enviable ability to compartmentalise. He could have a very satisfying night of passion and leave his apartment the following morning with a clear head.

Not so now.

He sighed and pushed himself back from his desk, swivelling in his chair to stare out of the window at another perfect summer day. From several storeys up, his only view was of the sky, a crisp, vibrant blue. If he went to the window and looked down, he knew what he would see. The uninspiring sight of people striding along pavements, hailing taxis, going places.

On the spur of the moment Elliot buzzed through to

his secretary. It took a matter of fifteen minutes but at
the end of it he felt immeasurably better.

All he had to do now was pay a little visit to Melissa
at the gym and fill her in.

Melissa had no idea who was waiting outside her door
until she finished her session with her physiotherapy client. Adam Beck worked at the gym too. He supervised
people in serious training, had a number of high-profile
clients whom he saw on a one-to-one basis, and addi-
tionally taught a number of high-impact classes. Melissa
had been to just one of his sessions and almost collapsed
under the pressure of it. She had afterwards laughingly
told him that he was a sadist in disguise and from that
moment on they had become friends, bonded by the fact
that they worked in the same building, were the same age
and were not at all attracted to one another. He had a
girlfriend with whom he was deeply in love and was
touchingly indulgent of her contented lack of interest in
any form of exercise. He spoke about her all the time.

Now Adam was trying to arrange something for the
three of them when Melissa pulled open the door and
was confronted with Elliot, standing outside, jacket
hooked over one shoulder, shirt carelessly rolled to the
elbows.

Surprise made her mouth drop slightly open. It was
one thing seeing Elliot at the apartment. She expected to
see him there. Even when he wasn't due back and suddenly showed up, she was always on the alert, every
sense tuned to the possibility that he might just walk
through the door, that he might be there when she and
Lucy returned from their workouts in the park. When,
weeks ago, he had mentioned his plan to chat with her
on a Friday about how things were progressing, she had
hoped that that would be the one and only day on which
she was forced to see him, but not so. Increasingly, he

had taken to just showing up. It puzzled her because it didn't fit in with the workaholic image she had tagged on to him and, after the first few bouts of heavy sarcasm, even Lucy now seemed to take his unpredictable movements for granted.

Melissa couldn't do likewise. There was nothing about Elliot that she could take for granted. Every time he was in her presence, she could feel her body prickle with an awareness she did her best to keep concealed. She tried hard not to stare, but her eyes would sweep surreptitiously towards him, and however much she attempted to maintain the cool, detached demeanour of a woman simply doing her job, he could still drag a laugh from her, have her hanging on to his every word, smiling at that dry, witty way he had with words.

He was being the perfect employer. He had stuck rigidly to his promise that no more would be said about that fateful night, and had done his utmost to make her feel relaxed in his company.

It wasn't his fault that she just couldn't relax whenever he was around. Or that her memories of him touching her kept her awake at night and still sent her imagination into overdrive as she concocted ever more wildly detailed scenarios in which he didn't just touch with his fingers... No, that was her guilty secret.

Now Elliot was staring at Adam, his lips drawn into a tight line, and Melissa was forced to make introductions.

'We work together,' she explained, plunging into the awkward speech.

'So I see,' Elliot drawled. He made no effort to extend his hand in greeting. In fact, he did the opposite. He thrust it very firmly into his trouser pocket and proceeded to lean against the door-frame. Physically, he was not as beefy as Adam, but he was taller and there was a leashed aggressiveness about him that made him appear tougher and more dangerous.

'What are you doing here at this hour? Is everything all right with Lucy?' She turned to Adam briefly. 'I'll get back to you about Saturday the 31st, shall I?' She smiled, but her mind was occupied with the man lounging in front of her. Normally, after she'd pummelled Adam, they would chat for a few minutes. Neither now seemed inclined to do that and of course Elliot was entirely to blame. He could depress an atmosphere without having to say a thing and he was doing it now.

'Well?' Melissa said sharply, once Adam had sauntered off, leaving her on her own with Elliot. 'How can I help you?'

'Sorry, but was I interrupting?'

'I *do* see clients during the day,' Melissa reminded him shortly. 'That was part of the deal, if you recall. I carry on seeing my clients and then devote the late afternoons to Lucy.'

'Yes, of course I remember the details of our contract.' He raked his fingers through his hair and stared at her.

What had she been doing with that man?

It was crazy to be thinking like this. In fact, so alien was the emotion that it took him a little while to work out that what he was feeling was good, old-fashioned jealousy.

'I have a proposition and I want to put it to you without Lucy around. Could you break for lunch?'

'Yes, but I have another client at two and I'm teaching a class for my old dears at three.' No way would she let Elliot think that it was fine to just breeze in and interrupt her day on the assumption that her hours were at his disposal, terms of contract or no terms of contract. It was trying enough dealing with him outside hours without the stress of wondering whether he might just decide to start popping into the gym during the day as well.

'These old dears…would they be roughly my age?' Elliot asked, pushing himself away from the door-frame and heading down towards the café.

'Are you in your late sixties?'

'Is it only you who teaches those classes, or are they shared between everyone? I can't imagine that body-builder chap teaching stretching exercises to the over-fifties…'

Melissa picked up the mild disdain in Elliot's voice and it didn't surprise her. A man like Elliot would have little time for someone like Adam, someone who didn't pursue a demanding intellectual career.

'It takes an awful lot of dedication to do what Adam does,' she said defensively. 'It's physically very gruelling.'

'Is that why their brains tend to be so underdeveloped?' Elliot enquired sarcastically. 'They devote so much time to making sure their biceps look just right that their brains wither away from lack of activity?'

Melissa held on to her temper with some difficulty. 'Not everyone needs to pour all their energy into making millions and running empires.'

'Not many can.'

They had reached the café, which at lunch-time was busy. It was a queuing system and sold the most mouth-wateringly delicious sandwiches and baguettes Melissa had ever tasted. For those who were feeling virtuous, there was also an array of salads, but it was a standing joke amongst the employees of the gym that most clients felt they had earned a few calories after working out. The baguettes were their biggest sellers.

Melissa grabbed a tray and tried to ignore the man next to her as she opted for a salad and bottled water. Not that he could criticise her if she chose to pile her plate with every form of carbohydrate on view. As far as Lucy was concerned, she was doing a good job. In the space of the past six-odd weeks, her excess weight was dropping off and her levels of confidence were rising accordingly. She had stopped moaning about school, had made a couple of friends and had even joined the netball team, which practised four days a week during the lunch-hour.

'You had a proposition to put to me,' Melissa said, as soon as they had found a table.

'I've decided that a holiday with Lucy might be a good idea. What do you think?'

'You want to go on holiday with your daughter? I think that's a brilliant suggestion.' She unscrewed her water, poured some into a glass and took a few sips. The salad stared uninvitingly up at her. 'Where were you planning on going?'

'I have a holiday house in the West Indies. It, too, suffers from lack of activity.'

'Would…would your fiancée be going as well?' Melissa asked casually. She had not set eyes on the other woman in weeks and it had not occurred to Melissa to ask after Alison. For a start, it was none of her business and she had been scrupulously wary of stepping anywhere near any subjects that could be construed as personal, and for another thing the thought of Alison only reminded her of that night when she had thrown inhibition to the wind and made a fool of herself, never once sparing a thought for the fact that the man she was flinging herself at was engaged. 'I'm not sure Lucy would relish the prospect of a holiday with Alison in tow,' Melissa added as neutrally as she could.

'She won't have to. Alison and I are no longer involved.'

About to dig into her salad, Melissa stopped, fork

poised, and stared at him. He'd uttered just seven words and she felt her heart skip a beat. 'You didn't say.'

'Was I supposed to?'

There was genuine surprise in his voice and Melissa rapidly worked out the reason for it. Elliot was not a man who accounted for himself. He had probably become so accustomed, in fact, to never accounting for himself that it would have taken a leap of indescribable proportions for him to have done so about this. Never mind that it was something that affected his daughter.

'You might have considered that Lucy would have wanted to know,' Melissa said quietly, and he frowned at her.

'Why on earth should it concern her?'

'She's part of your life. Everything you do concerns her.'

Elliot, at least, had the grace to flush, she noticed. It encouraged her to continue in the face of his uninviting silence. 'At the back of her mind she's been afraid of the prospect of being sent away to a boarding-school and she knows that Alison was very much in favour of that course of action.'

'Why didn't she mention something?' Elliot asked with a frown.

'I imagine because she thought that if she questioned Alison's absence it might bring the whole subject of boarding-school out in the open. She's only a child and, like a child, she decided that it was better to bury her head in the sand.'

'If you'd known about this, you should have said something about it. That was the whole point of our Friday meetings. So that you could fill me in on what had been happening.'

'I filled you in on…the essentials…'

'And I was supposed to guess the rest because I'm a mind-reader?'

Melissa looked at him stubbornly. At times like this, Elliot felt as though he had come up against a brick wall, and there had been many times like this over the past few weeks. Times when he had persuasively tried to lure her into discussing something other than work and superficialities, only to meet with the same silence followed by a swift change of topic. Every dead end only served to fire him up with a determination to break through the brick wall, to somehow find the way in.

'You're not eating,' he said. 'There was no need for you to take the salad just to impress me.' He watched her lazily as she immediately concentrated on enjoying the food in front of her.

'I didn't take a salad to impress you,' Melissa muttered, and he leant forward in an exaggerated parody of trying to catch what she was saying.

'Because you've worked wonders with Lucy.' He unhurriedly had another mouthful of his baguette. It was not his normal lunch-time fare but very good nevertheless. 'The thing is that you have completely different body shapes.'

Melissa gaped at him, taken aback by the sudden intimacy of his choice of words. Did he know what the effect was of what he'd said to her? Of his provocative personal remarks, which she had stolidly ignored whenever they had cropped up over the past few weeks? She had maintained a firm grip on the work front. Work and general chit-chat about impersonal things like what was happening in the news or the latest movie she had been to.

'Wouldn't you agree?' he pressed and Melissa succumbed with a shrug.

'People tend to,' she said. Elliot waited patiently as

she expounded on various body types and the efficacy of certain diets depending on shape and level of physical exercise. He politely allowed a few thoughtful seconds of silence to elapse.

'I mean,' he said, finishing his baguette and sitting back in the chair, 'Lucy is essentially tall and rangy. I suppose, having been blitzed with junk food, she's now getting back to her original shape.'

Melissa hung on to the slim life-jacket of relatively safe conversation being offered. She ignored the invitation to discuss herself. 'She's more settled now and, as I've said to you, it's because you're showing so much more interest in her. You ask her about her homework. She even told me that a few evenings ago you sat with her and did some physics homework.'

Melissa had done her best to restrain her hair. The curls were held in place with a no-nonsense tortoise-shell clip, but feathery bits still persisted in breaking free. Elliot found it highly distracting.

'I know it's wrong to say this and you must be very upset with your broken engagement, but Lucy will be pleased. I don't think she found your fiancée a very warm person. Perhaps it would have been different if she had been more at home here in England when she met her...' Curiosity was eating away at her and eventually she said, offhandedly, 'I thought you two were so suited to one another. What went wrong?'

'Nothing *went wrong*,' Elliot said briefly. 'Things went *adrift*. You must have been in a relationship that meandered?'

'Meandered?'

'Lost its way.' He restlessly glanced around them. 'As for being very upset...' He shrugged. 'These things happen. It's always disappointing when things don't work out the way you predict they will, but at the end of the day you move on.'

'What an uncomplicated way to live. It must be fantastic.' Melissa thought of how rooted she still was in the memory of their passionate encounter, a non-event for him that he had relegated to the past. Just as he had moved on from the disaster of a failed engagement. He was as cool and as composed as he always was. Not even a flickering change of expression marked any feelings stirring under the surface.

Elliot wasn't too sure whether he liked his life being described as uncomplicated. He had noticed over time that Melissa's criticisms were never overt. Instead her implications were quietly made and all the more forceful for it.

He met her wide gaze steadily and coolly. 'I would say so,' he drawled. 'Who wants unnecessary complications when simplicity will do?'

'You mean like the complication of emotion?'

'Call it what you will.' He raised one shoulder indolently. 'Let's take a hypothetical situation. Let's assume that I want you and you want me. How much easier would it be for us both to explore the interesting avenues that open up without the pointless complexities of analysing feelings?'

Melissa felt the warm rush of blood to her face and fought to keep her shock in check. Elliot played with words. He found it amusing to embarrass her and she could only suppose that it was because she was unsophisticated enough to be a novelty.

His brooding eyes gave nothing away. 'How can I assume that when we've established we're so obviously not each other's type?' Melissa laughed but her pulse was racing frantically and the directness of his gaze was causing her to squirm inside and visualise just what he was encouraging her to imagine. The fact that it was a hypothetical situation didn't make a scrap of difference. Nor did the fact that he was toying with her.

'Who's talking about type?' he pointed out. 'In this hypothetical situation, we're talking about sex, plain and simple.'

'Sex is never plain and simple.' Her cheeks were burning and her mind was scrambling to get a foothold on which she could steady her nerves. She was dangerously fascinated by the impossible scenario he was fabricating, even though she desperately wanted to dismiss it. She wasn't into playing these kinds of games, but…but…

'Never?' His vivid blue eyes swept over her speculatively and a shiver fluttered down her spine. 'That's where you're wrong. Or at least only partially right.' He allowed an infinitesimal pause before he carried on. 'Sex can be very simple but it should never be plain. But enough of that. Would you like some coffee before I get on with telling you the rest of my proposition?'

Melissa blinked and emerged from her dazed abstraction with a little start.

'Coffee?' he reminded her politely and she nodded, eager for him to be away from her even if it was only for a few minutes. She asked him for a latte, made some trite remark about it being a luxury she liked to enjoy once a day because it was so superior to the awful coffee she always managed to produce for herself, and then felt her body go limp as he headed off to the counter.

She couldn't allow him to get to her like this and she was angry with herself because this was the first time she had slipped up for a while. By the time she saw him coming back with a tray on which he balanced her latte and a black coffee for himself, her wayward nerves were firmly back where they should be.

She greeted him with a bright, interested smile and propped her chin in her hands.

'You were going to tell me about this proposition of yours to take Lucy on holiday. I understand if this means that you won't be needing me to complete the full term of my contract.' The thought of the job coming to an end left her chilled. She hastily reminded herself that it was a brilliant position and would leave her savings account bursting with good health. What more could she ask for?

'Not at all.' Elliot watched her over the rim of his cup as he sipped some of the coffee. He had seen more of this health bar in the space of two months than he had seen in the previous eighteen. He had also been less driven in his work over the past few weeks than he had been in fifteen years.

'In fact,' he said slowly, 'I think it might be an idea for your contract to be slightly more flexible than originally intended.'

'More flexible?' Melissa frowned and wondered where he was going with this particular remark.

'Do you have a passport?'

'A passport?'

'I can't stand it when you repeat what I say. How about just answering the question?'

'Yes, I have a passport. Why?' The light dawned. 'Ah. No. I really can't.'

'Why not?' He was prepared to spend a bit of time going through her objections, but in the end he was determined to break them all down.

'Because I have commitments here. You seem to forget that I still work for the gym. I can't just vanish for weeks on end at a moment's notice.' The thought of disappearing anywhere with Elliot in the vicinity filled Melissa with dread. It was bad enough having those

Friday meetings with him and they only lasted a matter of an hour or so.

'Employees have certain things called holiday quotas. Take yours,' Elliot demanded.

Melissa spluttered at the arrogant assertion. While she was busily working on an appropriate rejoinder, he stepped into the fulminating silence and carried on remorselessly.

'For a start, it's not a matter of weeks on end. It will only be for two weeks. And it's not at a moment's notice. In fact, you'll have three weeks' notice to give the gym, as I intend for this holiday to be taken during the summer holidays so that no school is missed by Lucy. But that's just the practicalities of the thing and those are the simplest elements to sort out. Consider this: it will be the first period of concentrated time that my daughter and I will have spent together. Yes, recently we've been communicating but it's been an uphill struggle and, were just the two of us to go abroad together, there's a very real possibility that all the good work that has been accomplished over the past few weeks will be reduced to nothing.

'In an ideal world,' Elliot continued, brushing aside any possible interruptions, 'Lucy and I would suddenly undergo an immense father-daughter bonding. Sadly, it's not an ideal world. More likely is that she will find herself cooped up with me and retreat quickly into her shell, from which she will nurture all the old resentments that have certainly not completely disappeared. She will feel obliged to converse and that obligation in itself will put immense pressure on her. I didn't know a damn thing about teenagers a year ago, but one thing I've discovered is that a teenager under pressure clams up, gets sullen and moody.'

'You wouldn't be stuck with each other all the time,'

Melissa pointed out. She didn't like the feeling that a net was closing in around her. 'You say your house is on an island. Well, there must be other people on this island, perhaps even people her own age. It's during the summer holidays. The whole world will be going abroad. Unless, of course, you've got your own island.'

'Which is accessible only by private jet. I use my Gulfstream.'

Melissa's mouth dropped open and she gaped. 'You don't, do you? Own an island? Have your own jet?'

'Would you find it more tempting if I did?'

Melissa considered the prospect of being trapped in paradise with a man to whom she was disastrously attracted, against every scrap of common sense in her head, with only his daughter as unwitting chaperon. She pictured a beach at night, deserted but for the two of them, unless she chose to confine herself to her bedroom with a book. She shuddered.

'No,' she said firmly.

'Good. Because I don't own an island and I don't possess a jet. I find that level of ostentation a little offensive, as a matter of fact.' He flashed her a complacent smile. 'So it'll be a normal plane to an island that is occupied by many other people. I'll get my secretary to book the tickets.'

'But—'

'No buts, Melissa. You're being offered a holiday abroad, in the sun, all expenses paid. You'll even be earning while you enjoy yourself. What could you possibly object to? Unless it's the fact that I'll be around…'

'No, of course that's not a consideration,' she mumbled faintly.

'Good. Then that's settled. You can break the news to Lucy when you see her this afternoon and maybe you two can go and do some shopping. That includes shopping for yourself,' he added. 'Put it on Lucy's credit card.'

'That's very kind but—'

'Why don't you just accept the offer, Melissa?' He stood up, waiting for her. 'You don't have to grind yourself into the ground, analysing the pros and cons. I've seen where you live. I'll bet my job that you don't have much of a holiday wardrobe to fall back on. Go out, buy some stuff for yourself. If you don't,' he leaned down to murmur in her ear, 'then I'll be forced to take yet more time off work so that I can drag you to Knightsbridge and assist you personally.'

Elliot knew the reaction his threat would evoke. She was, if nothing else, predictable in that regard.

He also knew that it would never have occurred to her in a million years that there weren't many other women who would have refused his offer to be equipped with an entire wardrobe for a holiday for which they weren't paying. And not many who would have seen his presence as a positive drawback.

He headed back to his office feeling remarkably light-spirited. It had been a while since he had taken a holiday. He hadn't been lying when he told Melissa that his house in the sun was suffering from a serious case of inactivity. He hadn't actually visited it for well over a year, although he had lent it out on several occasions, usually to friends with families. A housekeeper and her husband, who looked after the tropical gardens, were employed full-time to basically stop the cobwebs from staging a take-over.

He found himself wondering what her impression would be of the house. Favourable, he would imagine. Lucy would love it, of that there was no doubt. She might have taken her time to approve of him, but she certainly would approve of his holiday home. One out of two wasn't bad going, he thought wryly.

It would do him good to get away, he told himself.

And why deny it? He needed to get Melissa out of his system and there was only one way he could do that. By bedding her. He wanted her and he intended to have her because she was ruinous for his concentration.

She was wary of affairs, but she wanted him. He knew that and the thought was a constant turn-on. He felt like a randy teenager whenever he was around her. Of course, she was absolutely right when she said that they were not each other's type, but then hadn't he been truthful as well when he had told her that, in the face of lust, the question of types didn't come into the equation?

He was humming softly under his breath by the time he made it back to his office and set in motion arrangements for two weeks away from it all.

Which, when presented to Lucy several hours later, was an immediate drawback.

'But I don't want to go away,' she moaned, slinging her bag on the sofa and heading towards the fridge for a bottle of mineral water. 'Especially to some island in the middle of nowhere with a couple of adults.'

'Your father wants to use the opportunity to get to know you,' Melissa soothed, already writing off any thought of exercise for the day.

'He can get to know me here if he's all that interested.' The protests were the same but the tenor was different. Lucy was no longer fighting to the same extent. In the past month, she had begun confiding in Melissa, talking about her past, her childhood, her parents, and in some part reconciling events that had occurred with the circumstances as they were now. When Melissa had asked whether she could share some of her accounts with Elliot, she had shrugged indifferently but hadn't said no. Things had been progressing slowly and between Elliot and his daughter Melissa was a medium, aside from anything else, and that was the role she was to play on this holiday he had offered her.

'And it's only going to be for a fortnight,' Melissa encouraged. 'You can't possibly be missing out on that much in the space of two weeks.'

'I know, but…' Lucy hesitated. 'I'm just beginning to…you know…make friends and if I'm away…'

'They won't forget you.'

'They might. Besides, I don't know if I'm skinny enough for a bikini.'

'Well, I'm sure we can find you one of those old-fashioned swimsuits sculpted for older ladies,' Melissa said mock-seriously. She flopped down on the sofa and gave her a conspirational look. 'Your dad says I can take you shopping…'

'Well…I suppose it's only for two weeks, and there are some super things in the shops now…'

'Sure you can fit into any of them?' Melissa teased.

Lucy laughed and looked at her smugly. 'I guess I could squeeze into one or two things. The weight's been dropping off since I gave up the fried food and crisps and stuff. Course, I'm not as slim as I used to be. Funny, Australia seems like so long ago now. It's still all there, in my head, but every day little things take over. Is that wrong?'

They had had this conversation many times before. It had been traumatic losing her mother and stepfather, and then distressing having to move to England, to discover a parent she never knew she had. Now life seemed to be moving on, and that, too, was upsetting. Melissa always listened and tried not to give too much advice. As she saw it, Lucy had to come to grips with her changing destiny in her own time.

In a way, she suspected that it had felt more comfortable to Lucy to be swamped in misery, to feel isolated. Breaking out of that pattern and beginning the fragile process of settling down brought a whole new array of problems to grapple with.

She murmured all the right platitudes and continued listening as she prepared a light meal for Lucy to have later in the evening.

'Thank God you're coming on this jaunt with us,' Lucy eventually concluded. These daily cooking sessions were a valuable bonding routine, with Lucy chopping vegetables while Melissa did the actual cooking. Lenka's duties had been progressively refined and now all she did was the shopping during the day, and the cleaning of the apartment. By the time Lucy arrived back from school, she had already left.

'I'm sure if I weren't, you and your father would get along just fine.' She tasted her sauce and covered the pan with a lid, then helped herself to some mineral water.

'Yes, he would carry on working on his laptop and I would skulk around a pool pretending to be having a good time.'

'He's not an ogre and you know it.' Melissa grinned and leaned against the counter, glass in her hand. 'I mean, he's told me that I can go shopping for myself as well. Apparently he harbours the suspicion that my wardrobe might not be up to expensive tropical standards.'

Lucy was scathing. Who cared about keeping up with the Joneses? Who cared what was worn on holiday? Why did it matter if your clothes weren't expensive and designer?

Melissa heartily agreed. She'd checked her wardrobe and come to the conclusion that she could just get by on what she had.

And the last thing Melissa wanted to do was to draw

attention to herself while on this enforced holiday. She would do her best to fade into the background and make sure that she emerged only when Lucy was around, and even then she would not deviate from her safe role of assiduous chaperon, so to speak.

CHAPTER EIGHT

A HOUSE in the sun didn't go very far in describing the villa that was perched at the top of the incline, overlooking its own private cove.

Melissa, enervated after the long flight, gasped as she stepped out of the car and took it in. Thinking about it, she had spent the past few hours gasping in various stages of delight. She had marvelled at the first-class lounge, in which they could relax with drinks and snacks, away from the throng of people flooding the airport with pre-holiday hysteria. And felt in awe of the opulence of the first-class cabin on the plane, where the seats smoothly and miraculously transformed at the push of a button into fully extended beds in which you could sleep in a normal manner without having to contort your body into various unnatural positions. She had been almost overwhelmed at the heat that enclosed them the minute they stepped off the plane so that they could catch a much smaller island-hopper to the place where Elliot's house was. And now here she was, agog again at the sight of the villa that was spread before them in all its magnificent glory.

If Elliot hadn't already had the full measure of her lack of sophistication, Melissa thought, then he pretty much must have it by now.

To his credit, he had not been patronising. When she had rambled on at the airport about never even knowing that something called a first-class lounge existed, he had merely smiled and explained that businessmen found it quite a plus because it meant that they could carry on being dull workaholics in relative privacy. When she had

134

insisted on pushing the various buttons on the armrest of her seat on the plane, he had not looked away in embarrassment, simply pulled out a stack of files which he proceeded to review, leaving her peacefully to experiment with her gadgets. He had shown not the slightest hint of condescension at her amazement with her miniature television, which popped up from the armrest of her seat and which showed a choice of movies and television programmes.

'I haven't done an awful lot of overseas travel,' she had confessed, by way of explaining her overdone reactions to everything. 'As you've probably guessed by now.'

He had been unusually patient and understanding, and of course Lucy and Mattie, Lucy's new school friend, recruited at the eleventh hour to join their little party at Lucy's pleading insistence, didn't really allow time for much else. They had been as excited as two kids on Christmas Eve and had dressed for the occasion in small skirts, even smaller tops and platform shoes. They had chattered endlessly, helped themselves to vast quantities of muffins and biscuits in the first-class lounge, most of which they left, and took pictures of one another in various posed attitudes, much to Melissa's amusement.

'So, what do you think of my little house?'

Melissa drew her eyes away to look at him. After hours of travel, he appeared unfairly bright-eyed and bushy-tailed. And something about him just seemed to *belong* in this setting, probably because he was olive-skinned and faintly exotic-looking. She, on the other hand, felt dishevelled and greasy. She hadn't managed any sleep on the plane, despite the cunning fold-down bed scenario, and, while she wasn't tired, she still felt as though she looked like someone who hadn't slept for the better part of a day and hadn't had much chance of freshening up either.

'It's not quite what I imagined,' Melissa confessed. Lucy and Mattie were busy walking around, pretending to be celebrities, while the driver, who was apparently half of the duo who lived in the house and looked after it when it was not being used, was bringing their luggage out of the car. It was now dusk, but still very warm and the air was fragrant with the smell of various unknown flowers. It seemed silent, even though it wasn't. Insect sounds were all around them, quite, quite different from anything Melissa had ever experienced before. She breathed in deeply and Elliot felt his mouth curve into a smile. He wondered how on earth she could survive in the rat race of London with so few hard edges. The entire day had, from all appearances, been a voyage of discovery for her and she had made no attempt to conceal the fact. Right now she was inhaling deeply, head flung back, eyes half-closed, her face a picture of wonder.

'What did you imagine?' he asked, watching her as she slowly focused on him and blushed.

'Smaller. Less…grand.' They began walked towards the door and the moment for conversing was lost in the helter-skelter scramble of Lucy and Mattie as they stormed inside, chatting to the housekeeper as though they had known her a lifetime, then wandering off to have a look around.

Melissa wondered how Elliot could fail to be impressed by what he was seeing. Yes, it was his house and he had undoubtedly visited it many times before, but surely he couldn't be immune to its charm?

They had walked into an open area. Pale, marbled tiles were relieved with various faded, silky rugs, Persian in pattern and very well matched to the rattan furniture. It was not an amazingly big house, but it was very cleverly designed with lots of open spaces, so that the salty breeze could waft through and the sound of the surf could be heard as clearly as if you were sitting on the beach. The colours of the furnishings were pale, shades of oatmeal and cream and terracotta. Out through the sitting area, a sprawling porch surrounded the entire back of the house. It was to this that Lucy and Mattie had been attracted, and Melissa followed behind them, breathing in the uniquely tangy smell of the sea. The wooden porch was absolutely enormous, big enough to hold sun loungers, and down one end there was a long hammock stretched from massive hooks. In the background, Melissa was aware of Elliot talking to Lucy and Mattie, telling them a bit about the layout of the land, pointing towards a swimming pool that wasn't visible from where they were standing. She went and leaned against the railing, looking out towards gardens that were already shrouded in inky darkness. She could make out the shapes of trees and shrubbery and bushes and, to the right, the path that led down the slope to the cove which Elliot had described to them in the car on the way to the house.

Being here was unreal. It amazed her to think that a matter of a few hours could take her out of England and deposit her here, thousands of miles away, where everything was so vividly different. She was glad that she had swallowed her pride and gone out and done the shopping, which she had sworn blind she wasn't going to do, glad that none of the dreary, much-used summer clothes she had been wearing in England had followed her out here. This was a place made for bright colours. She sighed and had her eyes closed, trying to imagine what those dark shapes would turn out to be in the morning when the sun was out, when suddenly Elliot spoke from behind her, causing her to jump.

'Glad you came?' He went to stand next to her, propping himself up on the railing just as she was.

Melissa reluctantly opened her eyes. 'I've got no idea why you spend all your time working when you've got this at your disposal,' she said. 'Lucy and Mattie seem to have fallen in love with the place. I've never seen Lucy so excited. Amazing to think that she didn't want to come at first.'

'Amazing to think what you've done for her.' He turned so that he was now perched against the wooden railing, looking down at her, arms folded.

Under normal circumstances, Melissa felt that she might just have begun her usual edging away, but the air was so soft and musky that she didn't feel nervous at all. Thank you,' she said.

d that Lucy suggested inviting Mattie.'

laughed, relaxed. 'I know. A teenager's life is the potential for boredom even when there n things to do and see.'

f course, there's a computer around.'

g have you had this place?'

llio With light coming from just the g ov ad lanterns, Melissa's face was all ows and the breeze was lifting her ending it into tousled disarray. ce then it's been used a handful t all in the past couple of years. an's life. Enough money to buy not enough time to enjoy his pur-

Melissa laughed and sent him a life, isn't it?'

pathise.' He grinned back at her. He smooth those wayward curls from her face but instead rammed his hands into his pockets, where he could keep them safely under control.

'On the other hand it's your own fault if you spend every waking moment in an office.'

'Ah, back to what I know and like. Your pragmatic approach to life.'

'Simple approach,' Melissa corrected, 'and if I'm not mistaken you were the one to preach that piece of wisdom.' Her face warmed as she gazed up at him. 'You never said where Lucy and Mattie were. Is it safe for them to wander outside?'

'Absolutely safe,' he assured her. 'You're unlikely to find a safer place on the face of the earth. Anyway, they're not outside; they're in the kitchen. Merle is feeding them. Apparently, having eaten on the plane, they're still hungry.' He laughed softly without taking his eyes away from her flushed face. He felt as though every cell in his body was revving up, on full alert. 'Actually, I came to find out whether you wanted anything to eat. I suggest something light. There's fresh shrimp salad and bread.'

'Sounds tempting.' She sighed. 'Though it seems a shame to go in.' She pushed herself away with reluctance and gave Elliot a sheepish smile. 'Sorry. I'm not being very cool and casual about all this, am I? You must find it very amusing. Or annoying, of course.'

'Come on. Let us go and get something to eat,' he said roughly. 'It's best to try and go to sleep as early as possible, to give your body the rest it needs.' What the hell was he doing? Pandering to his curiosity? Filling his head with thoughts of seduction? This was a young woman, if not in age then certainly in experience. Yes, he found the novelty of that immensely appealing. Yes, he could think back about the way she had lain there, abandoned and eager to touch him, and his whole body would race in a surge of pure desire at the memory, but they were not in the same league. He was jaded and experienced. Just travelling with her had proved it, if nothing else had. Every new sight, every new experience had been a source of wonder to her.

'What's wrong?' Melissa asked worriedly. 'Am I getting on your nerves?' She almost added *already* but bit it back. They had a number of days in each other's company and she could see now how her excited reactions at every turn might have got under his skin a bit.

'Wrong? What could be wrong?' Elliot asked.

'You just seemed a bit tense, that's all.' She put her hand tentatively on his arm and Elliot felt his skin tighten. All his high-minded thoughts of bringing her to this paradise, seducing her because there was no other way of putting it, now seemed like the illusions of arrogance.

'Jet lag,' he said abruptly, nodding in the direction of the kitchen. 'Affects us all.'

Lucy and Mattie had already made themselves at home and were sitting at the large table in the kitchen, tucking into salad and bread while Merle talked to them about what they clearly had uppermost on their minds, namely what the town was like.

'We have dune buggies,' was the first thing Lucy said to Melissa, when she had swallowed a mouthful of food. 'Did you know? Mattie and I can actually drive into the town and shop around. By ourselves!'

Melissa had visions of two teenagers swerving around roads, but before she could open her mouth to voice a protest Elliot was telling her about the buggies, describing them, reassuring her that there was virtually no traffic at all. While he spoke, he filled her plate with salad and poured her some fruit juice.

The food was delicious. Melissa ate and listened to

Lucy describing the fortnight of high excitement she had in store for herself and Mattie. Intermittently, she would calm down and insert an appropriate statement about perhaps meeting Elliot and Melissa for lunch, which was her token effort at the bonding that Melissa had stressed was all-important. Mattie, by no means a shrinking violet, took up the excited monologue whenever Lucy decided to tuck into her food. They made an excellent duo and Melissa shuddered at the thought of them joyfully invading a sleepy little town in the middle of the island. It took her a while to realise that Elliot wasn't eating. He wasn't even sitting at the table. He was perched against the counter, watching them with a beer in his hand, while behind him Merle cleared dishes, obviously content that there were people in the place.

His reticence was all the more noticeable because he had been warm and friendly for the entire journey over, humouring her wide-eyed ingenuity. She wondered whether perhaps he had just got sick of being the perfect gentleman and was already bored at the thought of being surrounded by two giggling teenagers and a woman who didn't have the wit or sophistication to be at home amidst all this luxury, or at least to even pretend to be.

She made sure not to remark on the rest of the villa as he showed them to their bedrooms after they had finished eating. Their bags had already been laid out in the respective rooms, and Melissa left it to the girls to express their delight with the big beds, the softly draped mosquito nets, the blonde wooden flooring, the wicker furniture and the magnificent overhead ceiling fan. She herself kept quiet and did her best not to look impressed.

Her room was as big as the girls', although with only one king-sized bed in it instead of two. It was decorated with different colours as well, more greens and ivories.

'All the bedrooms lead out onto the porch we were

standing on earlier,' Elliot explained. 'It was designed that way so that anyone could benefit from stepping out of their bedroom directly outside.' He waited as she strolled over to the French doors and stepped right back outside onto the porch, though now from a different angle.

'Your luggage is all here ready to be unpacked, and there's bottled water by the bed so that you don't have to trek through the house in the middle of the night if you get thirsty.'

Melissa swung round to face him. 'And tomorrow?' she asked. 'What would you like me to do?'

'Whatever you want to do,' Elliot said irritably. 'This isn't a busman's holiday. You're here to enjoy yourself. You can go into town with the girls if you like or else you can relax in the cove with a book.' He raked his fingers through his hair, torn between wanting to leave and wanting to stay. Having always been firmly in control of the steering-wheel in his life, he suddenly felt as though he had lost his grip. For the past couple of weeks, he had been content to bide his time, having reached the decision that there was nothing wrong with seduction. He would not, he knew, be seducing an unwilling woman; that wasn't his style at all. Now he was asking himself whether seduction itself was desirable and the questions he posed himself made him feel unaccountably and frustratingly helpless.

He tried to match her even tone with a similar one of his own.

'Or alternatively, there are lots of beaches. You needn't content yourself with the one here. Ten minutes on the dune buggy and you'll find yourself on a coastal strip that belongs on a postcard.' She was reaching behind her, taking her hair out of its pony-tail so that it was displayed in all its unruly splendour. Elliot all but moaned. With great effort, he pushed himself away from the door-frame and curtly bade her goodnight, barely giving her sufficient time to answer.

Puzzled and depressed at Elliot's about-turn, Melissa went to bed and nevertheless slept soundly, awakening to find the sun trying hard to stream through the French doors. It was a losing battle. The curtains were thick and designed to block out light, even the iridescent light of the tropics.

When she pulled back the curtains the sky was cloud-free, and a high turquoise colour, and the gardens beyond the porch, which had enchanted her in darkness, were splendid in daylight. Every shade of green glinted in the light, and the flowers, neatly pruned back, were bigger and brighter and more extravagant than any she had ever seen.

Where was Elliot? She wondered whether she had imagined his coolness the night before. Was he regretting his impulse to ask her along? As buffer? With Mattie now on the scene, perhaps he realised that he hadn't needed her after all, but, having already bought her ticket, had been reluctant to cancel her seat and lose his money.

And to make matters worse, once Melissa had changed into some shorts and a halter-neck T-shirt, she emerged from her room, full of plans to make herself useful just in case he really was having second thoughts about his generosity in bringing her along, only to find that the house was empty. The girls and Mr Elliot, she was informed by Merle, had already headed off to the town to check it out, and would not be back until lunch-time.

Melissa had been left instructions to relax.

'Relax?' Melissa looked at the housekeeper, aghast. 'But I'm here to work! I have to...' She wondered what she really had to do. Certainly not accompany Lucy everywhere, making sure that no arguments broke out between her and her father, making sure that delicate situations were sidestepped. And with Mattie on the scene, their routine of exercise and walking was clearly not appropriate and even cooking healthy meals was a nonsense, considering Merle would be in charge of the food.

Which leaves me, she thought, slinking back into her room so that she could change into a swimsuit, an employee without a job.

She cringed again at the thought of Elliot brooding over the money he had spent on her ticket, not to mention the dent in his credit card, which he had generously offered to her and which she had stupidly used. Good heavens, she had been so wrapped up the day before, with her oohing and aahing, that she had failed to notice his reticence until it was staring her in the face! She had idiotically imagined that he was being the perfect gentleman because he was *putting up with her*! When in fact he had probably been groaning inwardly and kicking himself!

By the time Melissa made it down to the cove, she had convinced herself that, far from trying to be as useful as possible with Lucy, she should simply try as hard as she could to keep out of everyone's way. With a bit of luck, she could become virtually invisible. The gardens were huge. She was sure that there would be a number of trees behind which she could hide, and the cove would be useful as well. She doubted whether Lucy and Mattie would see the charms of an isolated bathing spot, when other, more crowded ones were easily within reach.

As for Elliot…

Melissa did her best not to think about him. She made herself enjoy the scenery, which wasn't hard, as it continued to be spectacular. The back of the house, with its expanse of shrubbery and open lawn, eventually came to an abrupt halt. A wall, criss-crossed with curling bright red and orange bougainvillaea, overlooked the sloping drop down to the cove. Further up, to the right, lay the path that wound its way down in a series of loops to the secluded bay. Melissa took this path, clutching her beach bag, in which she had a bottle of water, her suntan cream, a book, her towel and her sunglasses.

Merle had been vague on giving a definite time when the trio would be back.

'Lunch-time,' was what she had stuck to, and Melissa had realised that the single word could incorporate any time from twelve onwards. The pace of life over here did not appear to be dictated by watches. She decided that she would return to the house no later than eleven-thirty, an hour and a half from now. She would then be able to change into some dry clothes, adopt the appropriate attitude and try and work out how best she could last the fortnight without getting on Elliot's nerves too much.

The small bay was idyllic: a semicircle of pure white sand, as fine as castor sugar, and backed by shrubs, interspersed with palm trees, and the gentle incline of the hill on which the house sat. Looking up, it was impossible to see the house at all. It was set too far back into its gardens, and looking out there was just the sea, very calm and very blue.

Melissa neatly spread her towel on the sand, decided that reading would be a huge waste of time when it was just so much nicer to enjoy the beautiful views, and instead lathered herself in sun cream, protecting her face with her cap.

It would have been absolutely peaceful if her thoughts would leave her alone, but they continued raging inside her head as she tried to piece together what she could remember of Elliot's attitude from the minute they had met at the airport.

Had he been solicitous and indulgent of her obvious, gauche delight in everything or had he been quietly annoyed? He had certainly been cold when he had left her bedroom the night before, but had he been cold before then? And had she just not seen it because she had been too wrapped up in the wonderful novelty of it all?

The sound of the water lapping against the sand was like melodious background music. It was gentle and soothing and, with jet lag beginning to kick in, it worked its magic. The chaotic tangle of her thoughts and her futile attempts to try and put them into order began to fade away.

Melissa woke suddenly. Something had startled her out of her sleep. She sat up, horrified that she had nodded off in the first place, blinking into the bright light until her vision adjusted to the sun.

'You need to be careful. Falling asleep on a beach in the tropics isn't a very good idea.'

His voice came from behind her and with a muffled cry of surprise she twisted round to see Elliot standing above her with a huge canopy-style umbrella in one hand and a cooler in the other.

Even more alarming was the fact that he was dressed in swimming trunks and a thin cotton shirt that was unbuttoned down the front.

Every pulse in her body roared into life and she hastily stuck her sunglasses on, hoping that her bright colour could be put down to overexposure to the sun and not to the effect his body was having on her. Because it was a beautiful body with long, muscular legs, a powerful torso tapering to lean hips on which his trunks dipped and the flat, taut stomach of someone naturally inclined to an athletic physique.

'I'm sorry,' she stammered, standing up and dusting sand off her. 'I didn't realise the time! I meant to be back up at the house by eleven-thirty! Where are the girls?'

'Relax. They're at the Coral Reef Hotel.' He walked

over to her with the umbrella, which he began prodding into the sand at an angle, so that it was secure but resting on its side, providing some shade from the sun. Melissa watched him while he did this in mounting panic.

'What are you doing?' she asked and he stopped and looked at her with a wry smile.

'What does it look like I'm doing? I'm protecting us from the sun.'

'There's no need to bother about me. I'm just off to the house.' She stooped to gather up her belongings, aware that Elliot was still looking at her. In her swimsuit. It had seemed a modest enough bikini when she had tried it on in the shop, certainly a lot more modest than the ones Lucy had been urging her to buy, but now the frivolous black number felt indecent. She was aware of every inch of her exposed cleavage, not to mention the expanse of thigh generously on show, thanks to the minimally cut bottoms.

'You were sleeping,' Elliot pointed out, while she busily continued not looking at him and stuffing her things into her beach bag. 'Anyway, there's no point going up to the house. As I said, Lucy and Mattie aren't there.'

Melissa paused, hearing an implied criticism in his voice, but she really didn't know what her role should have been on this holiday. She was no longer needed by Lucy, who had a friend in tow.

'And I've brought us some lunch in the cooler.'

'That's very kind but really, there was no need to think of me. I'm fine being on my own. I mean, obviously I'll be around when the girls are here...'

Her voice dried up in the ensuing silence and Melissa licked her lips nervously. The breeze blew apart his shirt and she was given a glimpse of his chest, broad and well-toned. There seemed to be no way of avoiding his eyes without having to stare at his body, so she reluctantly looked at him.

'I could go to that hotel and find them,' she suggested feebly.

'So that you can do what?' He grinned crookedly at her. 'As luck would have it, they met a friend of a friend of a friend in the town and I should think your presence would go a long way to putting a dampener on their fun.'

'Oh.' Melissa sighed and wanted the ground to swallow her up. So now her charge was going to spend the holiday doing her own thing. Elliot would feel obliged to pay Melissa some scant attention, look after her because she would be on her own, while gnashing his teeth in irritation behind her back.

'There was no need for me to come along on this holiday, was there?' she asked quietly. 'I'm sorry. I should have dropped out the minute I knew that Lucy was bringing her friend along. My role originally was to be there as a buffer between you and your daughter, a third party to ease the way. I realise that I now don't have a role...'

In the middle of her speech, she was appalled to realise that he was walking off, fetching something from the bag he had brought down, which turned out to be a huge square beach mat that he proceeded to place under the umbrella. The matting on the underside was designed to lie flat on the sand but the top was soft towelling.

'Did you hear a word I just said?' Melissa asked, folding her arms.

'All of it. I just don't see the point of wallowing in self-pity. You're here and I suggest you stop feeling guilty and get down to enjoying yourself.' He took off his shirt and she reluctantly found herself staring at the flex of his muscles as he tossed it on the beach mat.

'I didn't realise I was wallowing in self-pity,' Melissa informed him stiffly. Now he had proceeded to lie down on the mat so that she had to move in front to see him. He had his hands folded beneath his head and his eyes were closed. 'I thought I was being open and honest and giving you a fair chance to tell me what a mistake you made in importing me over here.'

Vivid blue eyes met hers. 'Maybe it was a mistake.' She looked luscious. How he could have bypassed those curves when he first met her he had no idea because, when he looked at her now, that was all he could see. Her generous breasts, barely restrained by a top that was clearly meant for a less abundantly proportioned woman, her slender waist and softly rounded hips. Proper hips. No bones jutting out like those stick insects he had always dated. And a personality to match. Yes, it had been a mistake bringing her over. Brilliant idea at the time when he was nurturing thoughts of getting her into bed, but now he was retreating from that idea, definitely an error of judgement. He felt a stirring in his loins and sat up abruptly, shading his eyes from the glare.

'So you admit it, then,' Melissa said flatly. She turned away, her eyes stinging from hurt, and dropped everything she was holding. Without another word she headed towards the sea, away from him. She barely noticed the spectacular clarity of the water as she stepped into the shallows. The scenery just seemed to be swimming around her. With a choked sob, she waded out and then plunged in, lashing out without thought for safety, just needing to get as far away from Elliot as possible.

He hadn't been joking or teasing her when he had told her that her presence on the island was a mistake. He had been deadly serious and it was no consolation to know that only her prodding had elicited the truth.

She was aware of Elliot only when she felt his arms around her waist and immediately she began to thrash, first in the throes of her self-pity, then in anger. Anger at herself and at him. Out of her depth, though, she was no match for Elliot's powerful grip and eventually her flailing arms fell limp. They were both treading water and she was exhausted. She was aware of him pulling her back to shore and as soon as she could she stood and waded in, ignoring the arm still around her waist.

'I'm sorry,' was the first thing she said, when she was confident that she could actually string the words out without her voice cracking in the process. She pushed him away from her and didn't look in his direction as she walked tiredly up the beach, back to the wretched beach mat and the damned cooler he had brought from the house, stoically prepared to do his bit even though he hadn't wanted her around. It seemed he would grit his teeth and put up with her because he had no choice but to make the most of a bad mistake.

'It's an uncomfortable situation for you.' She took a deep breath and gritted her teeth so hard that her jaws ached. 'But obviously there's a way around this sorry business.' She gathered her things up and stared straight past him at some distant and unfocused point. She was aware of him looking at her, but she wasn't about to explore the concern and pity she would find there.

'There must be flights back to England. I can always get one.' Oh, God; eyes filling up. She gritted her teeth a little harder and took a deep, steadying breath.

'Look. I apologise. I shouldn't have said that.' Elliot raked his fingers through his hair and stared out at the sea for a few seconds before looking at her. 'Of course I won't let you go back to England...'

'*Won't let me?* In other words, I'm supposed to stay here, knowing that you don't want me around? Am I supposed to pretend that I've forgotten about that little detail while I get on with the business of enjoying myself? Would that make you feel better? Because you are, after all, paying me to be here so I guess the most important thing I should do is make sure that you don't feel badly about letting slip what you really think!'

'Stop this!'

'Will you arrange for me to leave? Please? I can't possibly stay.'

'No.'

'Then I'll have to do it myself.'

She turned to walk away and he reached out and circled her wrist with his fingers, yanking her back towards him so that she stumbled and collided into his rock-hard chest.

'You don't understand,' Elliot muttered savagely, keeping her right where she was, pressed up against him, both their bodies perspiring in the heat. She felt hot and slippery and she was trembling.

'I understand very well. I may not be experienced but I'm not dense. You don't want me here because there's no need for me to be here and what you're stuck with is someone you now have to be responsible for when it would be so much easier if I just wasn't around!'

'Is that what you think?' Elliot ground out. 'That you're a spare part? Yes, it is a mistake you being here but your reasoning is way off target.'

Melissa could feel her heart hammering angrily in her chest and she guessed he could feel it to because her breasts were crushed against him.

'You complicate things being here,' he murmured huskily. 'It's a mistake because I look at you and I want to do things to you.'

'Do things to me? Things like what?' In that split fraction of a second, she knew exactly what, then his mouth covered hers and his hand moved from her wrist to the nape of her neck so that he could lock her against him, hold her tight while his tongue did its devastating work, eliciting a shuddering response as Melissa stopped being held against her will and remained where she was purely of her own accord...

CHAPTER NINE

IT TOOK a lot of will-power to pull away so that she could look at him. He still held her, his hands on her arms, and she was glad of that because without that support Melissa thought she might have keeled over.

'I can't apologise,' Elliot told her roughly. 'I meant every word I said. Having you here is having temptation paraded in front of me.'

Melissa's mouth was still burning from where he had kissed her. The meaning of his words took a little while to sink in, then she blinked and looked at him in confusion.

'But...I don't understand,' she whispered in utter bewilderment.

'I mean,' Elliot brushed some hair away from her face and then let his fingers remain there, trapped in the wild effervescence of her blonde curls, 'by being here, you put me in the position of having to take too many cold showers.' The long fingers curved against her cheek and his thumb stroked the soft, peachy skin. 'Ever since that night at your flat I've thought about this, about touching you and, believe me, my thoughts have not been innocently confined to merely kissing...'

'Look...' Melissa cleared her throat. This wasn't happening. Was it? 'This is crazy...I mean, I work for you...I can't believe what you're saying...you told me yourself that I wasn't your type!' She was aiming for control but her body was letting her down badly. It was on fire and her breasts ached and throbbed.

'I thought I had a type. I was wrong.' He took one

step towards her and then proceeded to run his fingers along her spine, sending shivers of excitement racing through her body. 'If you really feel that you want to leave the island, then tell me now,' he said unsteadily, 'and I'll arrange it. But if you stay, I can't guarantee that I'm going to be able to keep my hands off you.'

Heady, reckless abandon filled Melissa's head like incense, blurring common sense and reason.

'Maybe I don't want to leave,' she sighed.

'Just *maybe*?'

'I don't want to leave.' She reached up and coiled her hands around his neck, pulling his head down to hers, closing her eyes as she initiated her own kiss and melting when his mouth softened against hers and his tongue found her probing tongue.

He had said that he had thought about her. She finally admitted to herself now that she had done nothing but think about him. She had been living in a state of heightened awareness, her body tuned in to the thought of when he might be around, when he might suddenly appear in the apartment. Fridays, the one day when she knew that she would see him, had become the highlight of her week. She had managed to keep her feelings under lock and key, had managed to focus on her job, but that was in England. Here…here there was no job to focus on, no lines of demarcation that she could fall back on, no sensible returning to her flat in the evenings and going to her normal job in the day, all those hours during which her head had plenty of time to subdue her feelings.

'Good,' Elliot said thickly. He pulled back but only so that he could lead her to their patch of shelter under the umbrella, then he was kissing her again, deeply and lingeringly, enjoying the way she squirmed and purred under him.

'What about the girls…?' Melissa asked breathlessly.

'Won't be back for a couple of hours.'

'And Merle? What if she decides to come down here…to get you…?'

'She won't.' Elliot grinned at her. 'Relax. There's just you and me and the beach and the sea.' He nibbled her ear and then kissed the side of her face, tugging her head back so that he could carry on kissing the delicate column of her neck. With his hand, he slowly peeled down the strap of her bikini, just one side, the side he could reach.

Melissa moaned. Part of her couldn't believe that this was happening. The other part wanted it so badly that she was shaking with desire. The slow scrape of the Lycra against her skin, as the bikini top was peeled off, was unbearably exciting and she trembled when finally her breast was freed from its constraint.

'God, you're beautiful,' Elliot murmured unsteadily. Her breast had the fullness of a ripe fruit and it was twice as tantalising. Her large pink nipple was swollen and the peak was taut and stiffened. He looked, drinking in the bountiful feast before him and then he could no longer resist. He grazed the sensitised peak with his tongue and felt her wriggle under him and arch up, proffering herself for more of what he had begun. Elliot smoothly positioned himself so that he was kneeling over her and rapidly relieved her of the remainder of her top, straightening up so that he could just take in the sight spread before him.

Last time he had seen her, sprawled naked on that makeshift bed in her flat, he had been stunned by the scale of her sexuality, so well camouflaged by her workaday clothes. But even then he had been under severe constraint. He himself had still been in a relationship and she had been under the influence of alcohol.

This time, he could enjoy her body. They were coming together in full knowledge of what they were doing. He intended to savour every last piece of her, very, very slowly.

Her full breasts pouted back at him. With one easy movement, he curved his hands around them and massaged them, pushing them up and rubbing the pads of his thumbs against the nipples. Had he ever felt this insistent throb of excitement in his life before? He couldn't think. She had extended her arms wide to either side of her and her head was thrown back, eyes shut, nostrils slightly flared as she breathed in jerkily.

He released a silent groan and bent so that he could lick and suckle at the rosy circles beckoning him. Tasting her was like tasting honey for the first time. While he gave his lavish attention to one nipple with his mouth, he played with the other with his fingers, rubbing the hard nub and loving the way she responded with shuddering enjoyment to his touch.

He had big hands and, even for him, her breasts were more than a handful.

Melissa tugged him up, but when she tried to touch him, he stopped her hand firmly.

'I don't think I have the will-power to make this last if you touch me there,' he muttered. 'And that's a first for me.'

Melissa smiled at him, eyes slanted teasingly, and instead ran her hand from his broad shoulders down to his waist. Then she slipped her finger under the waistband of his trunks and slid it along his skin, eliciting from him a groan of pure pleasure.

It was thrilling to know that she could make him feel just exactly how he made her feel, hot and out of control. She could read it in the fiery depths of his eyes when he looked at her like that, hungry and in need.

'Let me,' she coaxed huskily, and he breathed in deeply as she grasped his hard member with her hand, feeling its rigidity through the damp fabric of his swimming trunks. She began to caress and he squeezed her hand, stopping her.

'What are you trying to do, woman?' he rasped, putting himself well out of reach so that he could kiss the sexy smile off her lips.

'You just make me feel so good,' Melissa confessed huskily.

'Glad to hear it.' His voice was smugly pleased. He felt like a ten-year-old kid told that he was top of the class. 'What have I done that's made you feel so good?' he encouraged, moving lower and looking back at her through his lashes, catching the delighted glint in her blue eyes as they gazed back slumberously at him. 'Is it this, do you think?' He dipped his head so that he could once again circle her nipple with his mouth, suck on it, drawing it in and then flicking his tongue over the tightened bud, over and over until her breathing was coming in little gasps.

'Or is it this, perhaps?' He broke off to run his hand along her thigh. He parted her legs and then settled his palm over her mound, leaving it still for a few seconds before rhythmically moving it against her while he resumed his relentless assault on her breasts.

Besieged at every angle by all these conflicting physical sensations, Melissa lay back and simply enjoyed. She had never felt so wonderfully free in all her life. She was giving her body to him and the act seemed to liberate her from every hang-up she had ever had. A sigh of pleasure escaped her parted lips when he trailed his tongue over her stomach, down to her belly button, then he was skilfully removing her bikini bottoms, allowing her to wriggle out of them, so that he could continue downwards, taking his time to savour every inch of her and then breathing in the sweet smell of her femininity. She was, he discovered, a true blonde. He blew on the fair, soft, downy hair and then slipped his tongue into the crease. Lord, how he wanted to spend time tasting her. He had to exert every ounce of will not to let his body dictate a faster tempo.

Melissa moaned as his tongue explored her most intimate place. An explosion of pleasure started somewhere deep inside her and carried on growing as he slid his tongue along the throbbing bud. When she thought she could bear the exquisite soar upwards no longer, she was aware of him feeling the same, discarding his trunks, and then he thrust into her and began moving swiftly and firmly.

They came as one and for a moment time seemed to stand still as every fibre of her being roared into satisfied completion.

Their bodies were both slick from the heat and from their lovemaking as he rolled off her to the side, only to turn so that he could face her.

'I can't believe we made love on a beach,' Melissa said with a tentative smile. Now that the passion had ebbed, she wondered what happened next. So he had made love with her. Did that mean, she wondered with a sudden attack of nerves, that he would consider his appetite and his curiosity both satisfied? He set her mind at rest by gently capturing her face in his hand.

'Life is full of first experiences,' he murmured.

Melissa felt as if she was flying high up somewhere, on cloud nine. She wanted to share every one of those first experiences with this man lying next to her. It wasn't just about lust. It was all about the way he made her feel, the way he made her laugh, the way he made her think and see things from a different angle.

Later that evening, when the household had gone to sleep, Elliot offered her the chance of another first experience, swimming by the light of the moon and making love when the beach was cool, maybe taking along a bottle of champagne for company.

Over the next few days, Melissa tried to be as normal as possible when Lucy and Mattie were around, making a point of taking time out to wander into the town with them and visit the delights of the hotel to which they seemed to be drawn like magnets. On several of those occasions, Elliot remained back at the house, catching up with work on his laptop. She found that, however much she enjoyed spending time with the girls, visiting the beaches and seeing the sights, what few there were to see, she was always biding time until she returned to the house and to him, and he was always waiting for her.

And he was relaxed. He took them all out to dinner on a couple of occasions and even entered into the spirit of teasing the girls about their reasons for liking the hotel so much.

'It makes a change,' Lucy said airily. 'We're teenagers. Why would we want to be cooped up with two adults all day long?' This as the first blissful week was drawing to a close. They were in the hotel restaurant, a magnificent room with walls covered in colourful local paintings and batiks. Through the wide glass doors at one end, one of the hotel swimming pools was brightly illuminated with night lights and surrounded by gardens and palm trees.

'Because we're riveting people?' Elliot remarked drily, and they all laughed. He looked refreshed and utterly at ease. Every time Melissa found her eyes sliding towards him, she would make a concerted effort to look away, just in case the girls noticed anything. But it was very difficult. She wanted to touch him all the time. When they did touch, it was as if she was going up in flames, so powerfully did her body react to his.

'Maybe to each other,' Lucy pointed out, tucking into

her starter of shrimp with garlic sauce. Neither of them was looking at either Elliot or Melissa so they both missed the amused look that flashed between them. 'I mean,' she continued, surfacing after her first mouthful, 'you probably find it very interesting to talk about world affairs, but we don't.'

'And it wouldn't have anything to do with the fact that there are a number of teenage boys here, maybe at a loose end because they, too, don't want to be stuck all day with dreary adults?' Melissa grinned at them and didn't miss the sheepish exchange of glances.

'And girls,' Mattie pointed out, just in case the wrong idea was relayed. Four days into the holiday, Elliot had seen fit to give a small and very vague speech to them both on the need to conduct themselves in a respectable fashion. Listening from the sidelines, where she was curled up with a book, Melissa very nearly burst out laughing. She found herself having to translate everything he said into teenage-friendly language.

As far as bonding with his daughter went, the holiday was proving to be a huge success, even with Mattie in tow, which left relatively little one-on-one time as a result. Lack of stress, the lulling warmth of the weather, just being in the same place where time wasn't measured in the ticking of clocks, were all combining to soften the hard, driving edge that was so much a part of Elliot's personality.

But when it came to her relationship with Elliot...

It was something that Melissa thought about when she was alone and something which she avoided mentioning when they were together, because it was an unspoken question, the answer to which she already knew.

They were enjoying a holiday romance. Nothing more and nothing less.

He had told her all about what had gone on in his mind

during those long weeks when he had been formal and polite and scrupulously well-behaved towards her. He'd confessed in the heat of passion that under the surface she had been driving him crazy. He had even told her about his abandoned plan to bring her to his villa and seduce her. That had sent a delicious shiver of yearning through her and she had no doubt that he had been telling the truth.

It was all sweet music to her ears. How on earth could such a powerful and sexually exciting man see anything in *her*? She was neither as brainy as his ex-girlfriend, nor as skinny. When he told her that skinny and brainy didn't necessarily add up to sexy, she felt as though someone had given her a very unexpected gift.

But it was still a holiday romance. For him. He wanted her and he enjoyed her but beyond that no word was ever said. It was a thrilling present that led to no future and Melissa closed her mind off to the consequences of that because by now she was in love with Elliot. No holiday romance for her. She had found her soul mate, someone she wanted to share every piece of herself with, someone she wanted to spend the rest of her life with.

When did that all start? Melissa asked herself the question over and over, trying to pinpoint the window in time when respect for his cleverness but dislike for his arrogance had seamlessly merged into love for him as a whole. Yes, he could be arrogant, but he could also be gentle. Yes, he was supremely clever, but he never made her feel like a fool. Yes, she knew that she was a distraction for him, a break from the women he normally went out with, but when they made love she stopped feeling like a fill-in because he was such a generous lover.

And now the holiday was whizzing past and they had only a couple of days left to enjoy the island and each other. The days had begun to merge and the nights, when the girls had finally gone to sleep, had been theirs for the taking. The first experience of making love on a beach under the silver light of the moon had become three, although the champagne had only featured on one of those nights. When they happened to have the cove to themselves in the day, they swam and made love and swam and made love again. He told her that she did things to him and she treasured each of those remarks, keeping them to herself like a miser hoarded his gold, taking it out to inspect it when no one else was around.

Surely, she thought now as they finished their light supper in the kitchen and she retired to the sofa with her book while the teenagers washed the dishes, she meant *something* to him? Something more than just a fling? True, he had never said so, but Melissa, staring down sightlessly at the words in front of her, told herself that no man could be that solicitous without it meaning *something*.

'Penny for them.'

Melissa looked up from the book she hadn't been reading to see the object of her thoughts staring down at her. He was wearing a pair of longish khaki shorts and a faded tan-coloured T-shirt that made him look even more rugged and masculine. The sun had turned his skin even darker, far darker than she could ever get, although she, too, had noticed that her skin had become a golden colour and her hair was now blonder and even more uncontrollable. She had developed a habit of plaiting it, and it was plaited now, although enough of it had managed to wriggle free just in case neatness might be achieved.

He tugged the plait playfully and sat down heavily next to her. They never knowingly occupied the same space when the girls were in the house and she automatically edged away a bit.

'Oh, I was just thinking how well this holiday's gone,' Melissa told him brightly. 'The girls are having a wonderful time and you...well, you seem different over here...more relaxed...'

'It's a holiday,' Elliot pointed out wryly. 'People usually *are* more relaxed on holiday, and I have to admit, it's been a long time since I went on one. In fact,' he leaned back and tilted his head over the back of the sofa, his expression ruminative, 'it's been years since I took two weeks off in a stretch.'

'Maybe now that you've done it once, you'll need to do it again.' If it had been that long since he had taken a proper holiday, then he surely hadn't been anywhere with Alison, and he *had been engaged to her, for goodness' sake*! He may not have said anything about love or commitment, but surely that meant something? The fact that she had been the one with whom he had seen fit to spend a concerted amount of time?

And after that first day, when he had told her that her being here was a mistake, before he had explained his reasons for saying so, they had got along swimmingly. He was witty and sharp and fascinating and he had told her on more than one occasion that she was appealing. Appealing, she argued to herself, wasn't dynamite to her ears, but it was a start. She was in love with him and there was enough love inside her to make things work. Surely.

There was no denying that he wanted her. He made that perfectly clear when he touched her and sometimes when she caught his slanted looks they were hot with hunger.

Thinking about it made her shiver inside, and her pulses quicken. It was all she could do not to reach across and pull him towards her.

'Maybe,' Elliot answered the question she had forgotten she had asked, so wrapped up had she been in her thoughts. 'The girls want to go to a disco the hotel is having later this evening.'

'Later?' Melissa looked at her watch. 'It's eight-thirty now. How much later?'

'Apparently things don't get going until ten.' He shot her a lazy, seductive smile. 'Ten until one.'

This was the killer look in which he specialised. The long, speculative, veiled stare that could make her body burn. He had a way of looking at her, just as he was doing now, that made her feel as though he were actually touching her. She knew exactly what he was asking and her heart began to race. Yes! She lowered her eyes, hiding the burst of love that threatened to show.

'Would you need to stay there with them, do you think? Make sure they don't get up to anything?'

'I know the hotel,' Elliot drawled. 'There will be security everywhere, making sure that nothing gets out of hand. Don't forget, this is primarily a very expensive tourist resort. They can't afford to be associated with any wild parties or drunken teenagers, and I must say, those two have behaved themselves while they've been over here. No, I think I can return home and leave later to pick them up.'

'You're going to stay up until one in the morning?' Melissa asked with feigned innocence.

'I was hoping someone would manage to keep me up.' He briefly stroked her wrist with one finger and heat pelted through her like a burst of fire.

Her head suddenly cleared of all her muddled thoughts and she realised that with only two days of the holiday left to go, she was being given a chance to give him an unforgettable night, a magical few hours.

'Oh, right. Would that person be me by any chance?' There was a time when Melissa would never have thought that she could play these teasing word games with any man, but Elliot had changed that, just as he had changed everything about her.

'I don't see anyone else around here who could possibly fit the bill, do you?' He smiled slowly at her.

'No, no one else,' she murmured. Fleetingly, she wondered how she had managed to reach this stage, the point of being utterly vulnerable and in love with a man who saw her as fitting the bill right here and right now, but for how much longer? A man who gave magnificent pleasure, and not all of it physical.

Then she thought of a world without this man and it was like sudden darkness falling.

She would wait for him to return. While she helped the girls decide what to wear, she wondered what she would wear herself later.

Innocence seemed like a long time ago, she thought as she watched Lucy and Mattie parade a succession of outfits in front of her. They were on an excited high, chattering about who would be there, whether any other people not staying at the hotel would make an appearance. It took roughly forty-five minutes for them to agree on what they would wear, which seemed to be outfit number one in both cases, and then a further hour to get ready. The sun had turned Lucy's skin a wonderful shade of brown and she positively glowed. It was hard to remember the insecure, defensive teenager she had been a couple of months ago.

By the time Elliot had dropped them off and returned, Melissa was waiting for him in his bedroom wearing the most tempting outfit she could think of. Absolutely nothing.

They had never actually had the house entirely to themselves since they arrived. During the day, if the girls weren't around, then Merle was, or else her husband, who was the handyman and gardener. Or they were out themselves, at a beach with Lucy and Mattie, or having lunch in one of the excellent restaurants on the island. They made love on the beach and at night when the house was perfectly quiet, if not completely empty. Greeting him with nothing on was a first and the appreciation in his eyes filled her with a glorious, soaring sense of satisfaction.

'You take my breath away,' he said thickly, coming into the room and kicking the door shut behind him.

Instead of lights or the lamps on the dressing table, Melissa had lit fragrant candles, and the French doors leading out to the porch were open, so that the night breeze billowed the voile curtains.

She had left her hair loose, wild though it was, and the mayhem of corkscrew curls framed her face and trailed halfway down her back.

Elliot doubted he had ever seen anyone so beautiful in his entire life. Underneath those clothes, she was every man's dream. How could she not be? He moved towards her, slowly unbuttoning his shirt, never taking his eyes off her glorious nakedness. Her breasts were shadowy, succulent shapes in the candlelight. His hands itched to feel them, to feel her move sinuously against him in heated response. He tossed his shirt onto the ground and stopped to remove the remainder of his clothing, half smiling as her eyes were drawn downwards to his impressively erect manhood.

'Oh, no,' Melissa murmured, when he reached to pull her towards him. 'Not yet.'

She trailed wet, hot kisses along his chest, circling his flat brown nipples with her tongue. She had to force herself not to circle his sheath with her hand, so that she could feel it pulse between her fingers. She would get there soon enough.

Elliot breathed in sharply as he watched her blonde head descend the length of his body and he uttered a groan when finally her mouth covered his throbbing member. He coiled his fingers into her hair and flung his head back with a deep grunt of pleasure as she moved erotically, keeping up a rhythm that had him fighting for control. His eyes were closed as he fought not to bring proceedings to a premature conclusion, but his mind provided the powerful image of her down there, her breasts gently bobbing as she moved, her large nipples jutting out because he knew that she would be as turned on as he was. When she began licking his aching shaft, he could bear it no longer, and in one easy movement he tugged her up and then dragged her over to the bed.

'You witch,' he groaned.

Melissa laughed throatily. If she were a witch, her first spell would be to turn his lust into love, his desire into need.

'Lie flat,' he commanded. 'Don't move a muscle.'

'What are you going to do?'

'Nothing you won't enjoy…to the hilt.' He opened the drawer of the table by his bed and, to her surprise, brought out some red ribbons she had worn in her hair when she had first arrived.

'I wondered where those had disappeared to.' The breath caught in her throat as her mind grappled with the possibility that she meant more to him than he had verbalised, enough for him to hang on to the ribbons she had used for her hair.

Elliot didn't answer. With a glinting grin, he loosely tied her hands on either side to the bedposts. She could shrug off the silky fabric if she chose, but she had no intention of doing that. Instead she curled her fingers round the vertical wrought-iron posts. She was his willing captive, and when he began to explore her body she could only lie back and writhe in ecstasy.

Her nipples were hard, waiting for his touch, and she moaned deeply as he circled first one, then the other, with his mouth, sucking hard until it seemed as though a current of electricity had connected straight from her breasts to her melting core.

He loved her breasts. He had told her that repeatedly, had told her that their size and weight turned him on, as did her big, rosy nipples that darkened when she was aroused, which was always when she was with him.

Just knowing that turned her on even more now and he drove her mad by spending so much time there, sucking and licking and teasing the tight peaks with his fingers, rubbing them until she wanted to scream in frustrated pleasure.

With her hands out of the way, there was no guiding him as he savoured her. Instead, he pleasured her at his own leisurely pace, kissing every inch of each breast, licking below where the sensitive skin of the underside met her ribcage. It was exquisitely arousing.

'Enjoying yourself?' she dimly heard him ask, with a satisfied laugh in his voice, but she was too heated to formulate a reply.

He was straddling her, but as he moved lower, he spread her legs to either side of him.

The scent of her was wonderful, unique. As was the glorious, impassioned immediacy of her response as he delved into that most private part of her with his tongue. Her body arched up to meet his mouth and he plundered the innermost depths of her femininity, savouring the smell and the taste of her. When he felt her coming too close to her peak, he stopped, taking time to gently lick her warm thighs while she begged for more, then he would recommence his exquisite torture.

The only time he drew away was to apply protection, which he had used every time apart from that first day, when they had made love on the beach.

Melissa's body seemed held in excited suspension for those few seconds, as she waited for him to fill her, waited for the feel of him against her. He had become familiar to her even though each time they made love it was more earth-shattering than the last.

He entered her in one forceful thrust that brought a moan of satisfaction to her lips, then he began to move. He had come to know her so well, in the space of a scant two weeks; he knew how to move until her breathing became jerky and she whimpered for him to take her to that final place.

With no one in the house but the two of them, with all the privacy at their disposal, neither of them was hampered by a need for relative silence. She was aware of him huskily groaning, saying things to her that made her fevered pulses race as his movements became faster. Her final shuddering orgasm made her cry out and she freed her hands from their loose ties to clasp her arms around him, raking her fingers along his skin.

'God, woman, what do you do to me?' he asked, when their energies were finally spent and he had rolled over to the side. He propped himself up on one elbow and looked down at her. Tenderly, she thought, or was she mistaken? Was it just the ebbing of passion that softened his features?

'What would you like me to do to you?' Melissa murmured softly.

'Anything and everything,' he replied softly. 'We've two more days. A lot can be achieved in that time, although,' he added ruefully, 'the restrictions of making love on the beach are now very apparent.' He burrowed his face into her neck. It was a very tender gesture, but she didn't fail to notice that, as far as he was concerned, the time scale for them ran to the end of the holiday. There was no mention of anything after that and she knew that she couldn't press him. For all the passion of their lovemaking and the easy freedom of their days, there were certain things he kept under tight control. His emotions were one of them. He wouldn't appreciate her opening up the floor for debate on the topic of whether they had a future, just as he never discussed why his relationship with Alison had come to an end. She was his temporary and very willing plaything.

Elliot's *two days* statute of limitation left her feeling cold, but then to back out now was unthinkable, not that she wanted to.

She would, she decided, just have to be optimistic. Hadn't he told her that he had spent weeks thinking of her? When they hadn't even slept together?

Well, she thought to herself now, when they were back in England, he would think of her all the more, remember the times they had shared. He wouldn't want to break off their fragile, newly born relationship. Surely...

And she wouldn't put pressure on him. She loved him. Her love would be their glue. She caressed his head, thinking her thoughts and seeing rosy pictures in front of her, even though there was still that malicious little voice in her head telling her that she was being a fool.

'You're right,' she murmured, even though it hurt, 'a lot can be achieved in two days...'

Which went by with the speed of a bullet shooting through open space.

The villa and the sun and the carefree days seemed to fade into a blurred water-colour wash the further they were from the island, on their way back to London. Even

Lucy and Mattie, both unnaturally sober, slept most of the journey home.

Melissa tried not to let the yawning pull of reality affect her. She watched Elliot doze and dozed off and on herself, but her sleep was light and fitful. In one breath, she remembered what they had done together and told herself that he cared about her, even if he didn't necessarily show it. Maybe words of love and affection didn't come easily to a man as proud and controlled as him. In the other breath, she succumbed to the full force of facts. He had made love passionately and completely, but he had promised nothing, not even a relationship lasting a single day once they had stepped foot on British soil.

She would have to sway him, she decided, and the thought kept her cheerful all the way through Customs, and out into the crowded arrivals area.

Later Melissa wondered how long it might have kept her going if they hadn't cleared the crowds and spotted Alison standing to one side, immaculate in a pale blue suit, waiting for them, waiting for Elliot to arrive back home…

CHAPTER TEN

THIS was the time of day that Melissa was getting accustomed to enjoying most. It was six in the evening. Her parents would be downstairs, bustling in the kitchen, and she could sit up in her bedroom without interruption. She could allow her thoughts to wander freely over that disastrous final day with Elliot.

It was five weeks ago but it felt like only a few hours. She could see clearly in her mind's eye Alison standing there at the tail end of the waiting crowds, impeccably decked out, face smiling as she moved forward to greet Elliot. In that one instant, every resolution Melissa had made and all the hopes she had nurtured in her idiocy, to somehow get him to love her, just a little, just a fraction of how much she had grown to love him, had disappeared in a puff of smoke.

If Elliot had been surprised to see his ex standing there, he hadn't shown it. After a few seconds of checking out the new arrival, Lucy and Mattie had disappeared, with Lucy straight back to her old, sullen self, announcing that they would meet them in half an hour's time, leaving it clear from the belligerence of her tone that she dearly hoped that Alison would have left by then.

Alison ignored her completely, just as she had paid scant attention to Melissa. Good breeding forced her to be polite, but after that initial icy smile all her attention had been for Elliot.

Melissa sighed softly and stared out of the bay window of her bedroom. She was sitting on the broad, cushioned seat that could also double as a trunk, and had done when

172

she was a child, a storage place for all her toys. The view, as always, was inspiring. In her better moments, she took some consolation from the fact that nature just kept going, that her problems were small and transitory, really. Most of the time, though, she was overwhelmed by a huge sense of loss and a feeling that, if she had just listened to that voice that preached caution, she might not have found herself where she was now.

She might not have tried to insert herself between Alison and Elliot, horribly nervous but still reckless enough to try and fight for the man she had grown to love. She had hoped that her presence would remind him that Alison was in the past, whatever her reasons for turning up unexpectedly, that *she* was the present, the woman he had taken to his bed, laughed with, gone sightseeing with.

It had been a mistake. She hadn't banked on meeting the shuttered indifference of his response. She still shivered now when she thought about it, the way he had glanced down at her, his face cool and expressionless. It had felt like being punched and, though she had kept her smile wide and bright, her stomach had coiled into a small, hard, painful knot.

Alison, it transpired, had found out from his secretary what time he was going to be flying in, and she had arranged her day around the event.

Right to the last, Melissa had clung desperately to the hope that Alison's presence was all to do with business; maybe something urgent had come up and she needed to see him.

It was only when he had gone in search of the non-appearing teenagers that the full force of her stupidity was rammed home to her. Left alone with Alison, she had got the whole story from the horse's mouth.

Alison had explained that she and Elliot had never broken up in a voice that could cut glass. It was the voice Melissa imagined she used when reducing someone standing in the dock to size. She had simply got a temporary transfer to New York.

'I must be crazy to forgive him,' she had said. 'I know he's probably slept with you, but he's a man and men do what they do. You were available, I wasn't. And before I left for the Big Apple, it was an unspoken assumption that we could take time out if need be.'

'So you were no longer an item,' Melissa had pointed out, still fighting.

'Of course we were. We're made for one another. I'm afraid I did warn you against getting too close to Elliot. He's a very charismatic man and clearly one who took full advantage of an easy lay.'

Coming from that coolly sophisticated figure, the words were even more shockingly vulgar and Melissa had recoiled as though she had been physically struck.

The fight had drained out of her. She had wondered why Elliot had never been disposed to discuss Alison. Now she realised she knew. There had been no big break-up, no showdown, no anguished acknowledgements that he had become engaged to the wrong woman. Instead, Alison had been transferred abroad temporarily and while the cat was away, the mouse, put simply, had decided to play. She knew now that all the things he had said about spending weeks thinking about her, had been lies. He had just used the ammunition at his disposal. He had thought that he probably wouldn't have been able to get her into bed with a simple invitation, so he had persuaded her with golden words that had foolishly ended up turning her head. He had charmed her and she had fallen for it hook, line and sinker.

The scenery outside the bedroom window blurred. She could feel tears threatening and she swallowed them down. Actually, the crying was getting much better. At first, when she had arrived on the doorstep of her parents' house, she had been unable to stop crying. It helped that they had left her in relative peace, had been content to accept the surface explanation she had offered them, that she had fallen in love with someone and it just hadn't worked out. She had left out the details of their affair, of Alison, of her hasty departure from the airport, running away with her tail between her legs before Elliot had returned with Lucy and Mattie. She hadn't looked back. She had gone straight to her flat, cleared out her things and headed up to Yorkshire. A few days later, she had e-mailed her resignation to the health club and e-mailed Lucy with a vague excuse for her sudden disappearance, telling her that she had had to go back home for personal reasons but that she would be in touch as soon as she possibly could.

And as for Elliot…he still burned a hole in her heart. His image was with her every moment. She dreamt of him and woke up to continue thinking of him.

But time would heal that. There was no sign of it yet, but she was recovering. Three days ago she had begun scanning the newspapers for jobs.

She dragged her gaze away from the lilac, rolling views and glanced at the clock on the wall. In fifteen minutes, her parents would call her down for tea. They ate early and always bang on time. It was both frustrating and endearing.

She lapsed back into her thoughts and the next time she glanced at the clock, forty minutes had rolled by. Surprised, Melissa reluctantly abandoned the comfort of her bedroom and began heading downstairs. Maybe her little chats had worked, she thought with weary amusement. She had told her parents on several occasions that eating a high tea early in the evening was bad for them, because they invariably snacked later on before they went to bed. It had fallen on deaf ears, but maybe they had listened to reason after all and come to the conclusion that too many carbohydrates followed by inertia was a recipe for blocked arteries.

She met her mother halfway down the stairs.

'What's the matter?' Melissa asked sharply, forgetting her problems at the sight of her mother's flustered face. Her mother rarely got flustered. 'What's wrong? Is it Dad?' Her voice had risen with each syllable.

'You're wearing that old pair of jeans again,' was her mother's response. 'Why don't you go and change your T-shirt? Put something a little prettier on?'

'What?'

'And your hair's a mess.'

'My hair's *always* a mess!' Melissa shot back, taken aback at this line of conversation. 'And why would I need to get into a pretty T-shirt anyway?'

'Because you have a visitor.'

'Oh, Mum, you didn't.' Melissa had steadfastly ignored the teasing suggestions that had been popping up over recent days that maybe meeting a nice Yorkshire lad would be a good idea, to take her mind off things. Her mother had even gone so far as to mention a friend of a friend of a friend who had a son... The rest she had left tantalisingly hanging in the air and Melissa had chosen to ignore it. Now she felt a flutter of irritation and alarm run through her. 'Tell me you haven't arranged a date for me with whatsisname, because if you have I'm going back upstairs to my bedroom and locking the door.'

'I've put him in the "good" room,' her mother contented herself with saying, which made him sound as though he were a new stick of furniture, and Melissa groaned silently to herself. 'He's having a nice little chat with Dad.'

Melissa dragged her steps, following her mother down the stairs, past the little kitchen and the sitting room, and finally she became aware of low voices. 'I'm not going out with anyone, Mum,' she warned, just in case her mother was nurturing thoughts of fairy-tale romances. 'I'll talk to him because he's here and that's it. Understood?'

'There's no need to take that tone with me, young lady.'

She pushed open the door, which had been ajar, and, still frowning at her mother, Melissa took several seconds before she realised who the visitor was. This was the visitor who was too good for the sitting room, the visitor who had interrupted the punctuality of their tea time. And her heart stopped.

After five weeks, there he was, as cool as a cucumber, sitting down on the flowered chair and looking as though he belonged. Melissa turned away, ready to take flight but was firmly propelled back into the room by her beaming and obviously excited mother.

'Now, darling, your father and I have some errands to do so we'll leave you here with your young man.'

'He's not *my young man*,' she hissed virulently, watching in dismay as her father stood up and shook hands with Elliot.

Good lord, Elliot was even more fabulous in the flesh than she remembered. With impeccable manners, he stood up as well and came across to her mother to deposit a kiss on one receptive cheek.

Then her parents were going, leaving, deserting her. She heard the front door slam shut and the silence wrapped itself around her like a vice.

'What are you doing here?' Her voice was icy cold and filled with loathing.

'What do you think? That I was just passing by so I thought I'd drop in? I came to see you.'

'Well, I don't want to see you! I want you to leave! Right now!' She had backed away from the threat of him and was pressed against the wall, trembling, not daring to look at him in case that old familiar weakness set in again. But she could feel all the masculine energy emanating from him in waves and pooling around her. Behind her back she clenched her open palms into fists, until her fingernails bit into her skin.

The weather had cooled as summer turned into autumn and he was wearing a pair of faded jeans and a sweatshirt. Out of the corner of her eye, she could see his leather jacket on the upright chair at the side, beaten brown leather.

'I'm not leaving, Melissa.'

'My parents shouldn't have let you in! How did you find me?'

'You told me roughly where they lived. I made a few calls. For God's sake, woman, why don't you go and sit down and stop standing there as though you're in mortal terror of me?'

Melissa scuttled over to the sofa and collapsed onto it, drawing her feet up and tucking them under her. Her heart was beating like a sledgehammer in her chest. She was aware of him sitting down on the sofa at the other end and she could feel the hesitancy in his silence. She had no idea why he had come but she had her suspicions, and if he thought that he could revive any kind of sexual relationship between them then he was in for a shock.

'Lucy misses you,' he said eventually, at which point Melissa finally looked at him, noticing for the first time that his face seemed drawn and there were lines of tiredness etched by his eyes.

He hadn't come for her, she thought numbly. There

she went again, imagination running riot and in all the wrong directions, reading messages that weren't there. He had come because of his daughter. Her emotions went into deep freeze as this slice of bitter reality presented itself to her. She made herself look at him squarely in the eyes.

'I'm sorry. How is she?'

'Subdued since you left.' He raked his fingers through his hair and rubbed his eyes with his thumbs. 'She blames me, of course.'

'And of course we can't have *that*, can we?' Melissa asked with cutting sarcasm. Anger gave her strength. 'I mean, *heaven forbid* that the great and wonderful Elliot Jay should ever be blamed for anything!'

His mouth tightened and she could sense him holding himself back. Why? Because, she thought with vicious clarity, he knew that he was on the back foot. Even *he* must be aware of how she had felt at the airport five weeks ago, when he had looked at her as if she were a stranger instead of someone he had shared the most intimate moments with!

He wanted to retaliate, probably give her another of his famous speeches on living for the moment or whatever, but he couldn't because he was here to ask a favour of her.

'I'm not going back. I'm sorry Lucy misses me. I miss her, too, but I'm here now and here is where I'm going to stay.'

'Why?' He slanted her a look of burning intensity, his blue eyes settling on her face until she felt her insides begin to squirm. More than anything else, she hated herself for that, for reacting to him even when she knew him for what he was.

'Because I've realised that I'm not cut out for life in the big city. I'm a small-town girl and a small town is where I belong.' She thought of the excitement and buzz of London, and then of the Yorkshire lad waiting round the corner and maybe getting a job twenty minutes away, returning home in the evening for tea with her parents until she found someone and settled down. Except, after Elliot, she wasn't sure there ever would be that someone. Who could ever survive the comparisons?

'I'm sorry.'

'Don't. Just don't. I don't want you feeling sorry for me. In fact, I don't want you here at all. I'm not going back so that I can be used to smooth things over with your daughter. You'll just have to enlist the help of your fiancée for that.'

'I don't feel sorry for you,' Elliot said brusquely. He stood up and began pacing the room. 'And there's no fiancée.'

'Oh, right. Does Alison know that?'

Elliot paused in his restless pacing to look at her narrowly. 'Alison has known that for several months.'

'Really? Pull the other one.'

'Meaning?'

Melissa inhaled deeply and decided to let him have it or be damned. 'Meaning that you led me to believe that you and Alison had broken up. OK, you didn't seem keen to go into the details and I only discovered why later. Because, according to Alison, there had *been* no break-up. She had been transferred temporarily to New York, but basically she was coming back. That was why she came to the airport. To meet you. I thought…'

'Carry on,' Elliot said expressionlessly. 'I'm interested to see where this is going.'

'I don't know what I thought…' Melissa muttered.

'You thought that, after what we shared, I should have said something at the airport. Should have at the very least put my arms around you, staked my priorities?'

Put like that, it sounded pathetic, so she remained silently miserable. She couldn't even react when he moved across to the sofa and sat down, closer to her this time.

'I should have,' he said in a low voice, and Melissa reluctantly looked at his strong, handsome face, for once vulnerable and hesitant. She absolutely refused to allow hope to find a way into her heart. She had been used and that was all there was to it. And here he was, using a few smooth words so that he could use her again. No chance.

'Why?' she threw at him bitterly. 'Why should you have? When you already knew where your priorities lay?'

'With Alison? If you really believe that I'm the type of man who has a casual fling with a woman for no better reason than his fiancée happens to be out of town, then tell me now and I'll walk away from this house and it'll be the last time you see me.'

He stood up when Melissa stubbornly maintained her silence. It was only as he reached the door that she looked at him and allowed herself to contemplate the reality of him disappearing out of her life forever. No, she had already lived through that. But for him to vanish on this ugly note...how could she ever live with herself again? At least, she thought, she would speak her mind the best she could, and now that he had refuted her assumptions, did she really believe him to be an out-and-out two-timing bastard? The answer was no. He'd just indulged in, what was for him, a disposable relationship. The fact that she had wanted more was her fault, not his.

'I was only repeating what she told me at the airport,' Melissa said. 'And it made sense,' she continued, as he paused by the door to hear her out, 'when you could barely meet my eyes.'

'You haven't answered me. Do you believe me to be the type of man who uses women?'

'Yes,' Melissa said honestly, 'but not two at the same time.' If he didn't like that answer, then he could leave. It was the truth. But if he left…her eyes glazed over with tears and she looked down hastily. She wasn't aware of him until he was kneeling in front of her, pulling out a handkerchief, which she accepted while informing him in a shaky voice that she wasn't crying.

'Why didn't you?' she asked, stumbling over her words and hating herself for even asking the question. 'Why didn't you see how rejected you made me feel when you just stood there, ignoring me? After those wonderful two weeks we'd spent together?'

'I'm sorry,' Elliot whispered, shoving her over so that he could sit right next to her and pull her against him. 'I suppose I was…'

'Was *what*?' Melissa whispered harshly.

'Afraid.'

Melissa pulled back to look at him uncertainly. 'Afraid of what?' she asked in a voice that indicated *pull the other one*.

'There I was. I'd just had the two greatest weeks of my life, and suddenly I'm confronted by a clash of realities. There was no question of Alison being a part of my life, but she did represent everything I had ever known in all my relationships. Order, predictability, restraint. And then there was you, impulsive, joyous, unpredictable. For a moment I wondered where the hell I belonged.'

The two greatest weeks of his life. Melissa focused on that little phrase and, while she marvelled at it, hope slipped in unnoticed and lodged somewhere in her heart.

Belatedly she remembered that this was the man who had kept well away from her for the past five weeks and had only shown up because his daughter missed her and he was having to cop the blame for it. She winced at the feel of his hard chest and tugged back so that she could resume some necessary distance.

'And there's no need to tell me what choice you made. What a shame you've had to find yourself here now, because Lucy's forced your hand.'

'No one forces my hand,' Elliot said softly. He reached to wipe dry the damp trail of a tear with his thumb and Melissa jerked back. 'Yes, I haven't seen you for five weeks and they have been the worst five weeks of my life.'

He waited for that to sink in, but Melissa stared back at him with mutinous disbelief. He really couldn't blame her, but God he wanted to hold that soft, frowning face between his hands and kiss it until the sun rose again and her wonderful smile emerged.

'I had to think,' he said flatly. 'Something had happened to me and I found that I couldn't deal with it.'

'Right.' *Lucy had reinstated war zones and he no longer had a useful buffer to oil his path.*

'For the first time ever I found myself standing on quicksand and that's why I had to come here. I thought I could rein things back to normality, told myself that if you walked out of my life then perhaps it was for the best because I could resume the life I had always known. I was wrong. I discovered that, actually, I couldn't live without you and I didn't want to.'

'But…you don't mean that… Alison said…'

'Alison lied. I broke off that relationship the day after I went to your flat. Another memorable evening.' He gave her a crooked smile and she flushed. 'On the back of that, she accepted a transfer abroad that, it transpired, didn't work out. She showed up at the airport because she wanted me back and she wanted to make sure that you knew. I haven't seen her since that day. Another man would have rushed to you, but I have never been one…'

He sighed deeply and expressively and Melissa risked stroking his face gently. He caught her hand in his and kissed her open palm. 'I find that I don't want to spend another day without you,' he said hoarsely. 'I love you. I don't know when it started and I'm not sure how it slipped in, but I do. Madly, deeply and for all eternity.'

There was a wonderful singing in her ears. 'You love me?' she asked. 'Me? You? Love?'

'And I know what you're going to say.'

'You do?' This came as something of a shock since *she* didn't know what she was going to say!

'And I agree. Nothing less than marriage will do. So…will you marry me?'

'Marry you?'

Taken aback by the quietness of her response, Elliot was gripped by a ferocious sense of urgency. 'Marry me,' he confirmed roughly. 'And there'll be no long engagement either. I want you with me as soon as possible. If I had my way,' he grated forcefully, 'it would be tonight, but I don't suppose the local registrar's office will still be open. And anyway,' he added for good measure, 'I know your parents would like something a little bigger and a little more church-oriented.'

'They *said that*?'

'They did,' Elliot told her smugly. 'After I told them how much I loved their daughter and asked your father for your hand in marriage. I also told them what a great husband I would make.'

Melissa laughed. She felt as though she was flying, really soaring, and there were no doubts and no inner voices waiting to clip her wings.

'Well, then, considering I absolutely adore you, too, I guess a church wedding is what it will have to be.'

'And in the meantime,' Elliot took a small box from his pocket and withdrew a ring from it, 'just to make sure that the world knows you're mine…' He slipped it onto her finger. It was a perfect fit.

'It's beautiful—' more tears threatened '—not that the world would think anything but that I'm a woman in love forever, with or without a ring…'

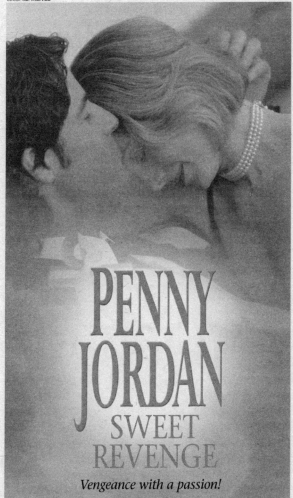

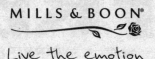

4 FREE

BOOKS AND A SURPRISE GIFT!

We would like to take this opportunity to thank you for reading this Mills & Boon® book by offering you the chance to take FOUR more specially selected titles from the Modern Romance™ series absolutely FREE! We're also making this offer to introduce you to the benefits of the Reader Service™—

- ★ FREE home delivery
- ★ FREE gifts and competitions
- ★ FREE monthly Newsletter
- ★ Exclusive Reader Service offers
- ★ Books available before they're in the shops

Accepting these FREE books and gift places you under no obligation to buy, you may cancel at any time, even after receiving your free shipment. Simply complete your details below and return the entire page to the address below. You don't even need a stamp!

YES! Please send me 4 free Modern Romance books and a surprise gift. I understand that unless you hear from me, I will receive 6 superb new titles every month for just £2.75 each, postage and packing free. I am under no obligation to purchase any books and may cancel my subscription at any time. The free books and gift will be mine to keep in any case.

P5ZED

Ms/Mrs/Miss/Mr ....Initials ....

BLOCK CAPITALS PLEASE

Surname ....

Address ....

....

....Postcode..

Send this whole page to:
UK: FREEPOST CN81, Croydon, CR9 3WZ